*Two rebellious cousins—and
the men who tame them!*

Meet Caitlin and Maddie: two beautiful,
spirited cousins seeking to overcome family
secrets and betrayal....

Neither cousin is looking for marriage—these Texas
women have proud, rebellious hearts, and it would
take two very powerful men to tame them.

But look out, Caitlin and Maddie—two tough,
gorgeous guys are about to try to sweep you up the
aisle...and they won't take no for an answer!

These two rebel brides are about to
meet their match at last.
Last month we met Caitlin in
**To Claim a Wife** (#3556)

This month enjoy Maddie's story in
**To Tame a Bride** (#3560)

Dear Reader,

I grew up watching Roy Rogers movies. Dale Evans, his costar who later became his wife, often played a spirited, sometimes spoiled heroine who started out being a trial to this noble Western hero before he won her over and she fell in love with him. A little like Linc and Maddie in my story.

Roy Rogers was my first crush. My lifelong admiration for this kind, gentle man, who was the same man of honor in real life that he played on the screen, has strongly influenced the ranch stories I love to write.

I hope you enjoy Linc and Maddie's story. I had a ball writing about these two.

Happy trails to the King of the Cowboys; and to Dale, God bless you and keep you with us. For the rest of you, I hope your lives are filled with happily-ever-afters.

# To Tame a Bride
## Susan Fox

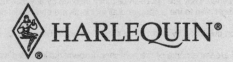

HARLEQUIN®

TORONTO • NEW YORK • LONDON
AMSTERDAM • PARIS • SYDNEY • HAMBURG
STOCKHOLM • ATHENS • TOKYO • MILAN • MADRID
PRAGUE • WARSAW • BUDAPEST • AUCKLAND

For my mother, Marvel Terry. The sweetest, most loving mother on planet Earth, and the gentlest, classiest, most honorable woman I know. I love you with all my heart. I can't find adequate words to express how much you mean to me. God bless you.

ISBN 0-373-03560-8

TO TAME A BRIDE

First North American Publication 1999.

Copyright © 1999 by Susan Fox.

# CHAPTER ONE

THAT FRIDAY MORNING, Madison St. John almost missed her mother's phone call.

She'd been on her way out the door for a shopping trip when she heard the phone ring. Because the maid would answer and take a message, Madison ignored it and walked on to her car.

Few people made personal calls to Madison St. John. She had no family besides her absent mother and a cousin, Caitlin Bodine. She and Caitlin hadn't spoken in five years, and her mother only contacted her on the rare occasion that she recalled she had a daughter.

Infrequent Christmas and birthday gifts were Madison's only proof that her mother gave a thought to her at all. Gifts which often arrived in the wrong month, indicating both a conscience that ran on delay and an uncertainty of just which month her mother had given birth. Judging by the age-appropriateness of the gifts, Rosalind St. John was also behind in her calculation of the year her only child had been born.

Madison didn't know if her devil-may-care father had survived the European racing circuit or his bohemian lifestyle. She'd been twelve years old the last time she'd heard from him. He'd sent her a postcard from some obscure village in France, but that was eleven years ago now. She had no idea if her mother had been in more recent contact with the jet-setting

playboy she'd been married to so briefly once upon
a time, or if he was even alive. Whatever had become
of him, it wasn't something Madison would likely
ever know, unless she bothered to hire an investigator.

Madison suppressed the dismal thoughts. She'd
lived most of her life without her mother and father,
and she could go on doing so. She'd learned to need
no one, and there were times when she was glad of
it. Life was so much less painful if you didn't care
about anyone.

The chauffeur had just opened the back door of her
Cadillac when the maid bustled out of the mansion
and rushed down the sidewalk toward her.

"Miss St. John!"

Madison turned her head, annoyed by the delay.
The little maid was in the kind of haste Madison considered undignified, and the faint scowl she gave the
woman was meant to convey that. This maid had only
worked for her three months, but by now she should
have learned how Madison expected her to conduct
herself.

The maid's excited, "Miss St. John—you have a
call—your mother!" betrayed a knowledge of things
the woman shouldn't have been privy to.

Though Madison rarely discussed her background
with anyone—and *never* with her staff—this sign that
the maid knew precisely how rare and significant such
a call would be was evidence that Madison's employees, like everyone else in Coulter City, Texas,
gossiped about her behind her back. She arched a
brow and stared coolly until the little maid's eyes
veered guiltily from hers.

Her stiff, "Thank you, Charlene," was rigidly

composed, as was her ladylike stride as she stepped away from her car and walked back to the mansion.

Her heart did a little flip as the news of her mother's call began to impact her more deeply. Memories of her childhood flashed strongly through her mind. She'd been devoted to her glamorous mother, doing anything she could to please her. Because her handsome, dashing father was around so infrequently, her mother was often sad and at loose ends.

Madison had desperately wanted her mother to be happy. Rosalind could be so bright and cheery and fun that her gloomy moods were frightening for her small daughter. Hadn't Madison known, even then, that she would lose her mother if she couldn't cure Rosalind's unhappiness?

She'd tried so hard to please her distracted parent. She'd been her mother's slave and her shadow, fetching things for her, never causing problems, keeping her own little dresses clean and her hair neat. It had terrified Madison to discover that she was an ugly duckling, but she'd heard her mommy complain about it to her friends, so it had to be true. The tone of her mother's voice when she'd said the words had made her feel sick to her stomach. She'd realized then how lucky she was that anyone bothered with her at all; she also learned that her value to the people she loved and needed most rested almost completely on her looks.

Each night she'd asked God to make her beautiful so her mother could love her. If God made her beautiful, perhaps her handsome father would come home, or he'd send them plane tickets so they could fly to France and watch him race his cars.

Every morning she'd gotten up and dashed to the mirror to see if her prayers had been answered. Every morning she'd had to face the same homely little features and dishwater-blond hair that she'd gone to bed with the night before.

Though it had broken her heart, she'd understood how unfair it was that a woman as beautiful as her mother had been left alone to raise a homely little girl. She'd worried about how embarrassing it must be for Rosalind to be seen with her, and to have to present such an ugly child to her glamorous friends— whose own children were so pretty and hand-some...and cruel.

Her worst fears came true the summer she turned eight. She'd known then that it was too late; her mother had waited long enough for her ugly duckling to show some sign of becoming a swan. Rosalind St. John had taken Madison to her grandmother, Clara Chandler, introduced her to the elderly woman whom she'd never met, then abandoned her to her grand-mother's dour mercies.

As an adult, Madison understood how crippling her childhood had been, how desolate and misguided. Living with her grandmother had been a new little hell of its own. But through her grandmother, she'd gotten to meet her country cousin, Caitlin Bodine. Though dark-haired Caitlin was as beautiful as a little angel, she'd never seemed to notice that Madison was homely. She never made fun of her face or her hair, never was mean to her in any way.

Caitlin's mother had just died and her father didn't care about her either. With so much in common, they'd bonded to each other instantly. Madison had been so grateful for Caitlin's unconditional friendship that she'd cried herself to sleep with happiness every night that first week.

Madison blinked away the sentimental sting. Caitlin... The painful moral dilemma she'd been wrestling with for weeks sent another wave of chaos through her heart. Could she truly forgive her cousin and dearest friend for what she'd done? Only the distraction of her mother's phone call could have quieted that chaos and given her a strong enough focus to ignore it.

She walked into the library and paused to close the door. The moment she was certain she was alone, she dashed across to the big desk and snatched up the telephone receiver. She hesitated before she spoke, squeezing her eyes closed, trying to moderate her excited breaths to sound completely normal and composed. Her pulse rate accelerated until her heart battered her chest.

Her quiet, "Madison St. John," was as unaffected as she could make it. She gripped the phone receiver so tightly that her fingers ached.

"Hello, Maddie! My goodness, you sound so grown-up—how *are* you, dear?"

Rosalind's question was a practised social opener, not one she seriously wanted an answer to. Madison forced a smile into her voice and came right back with a saccharine, "How are *you*, Mother? You sound wonderful."

"I've remarried," Rosalind burst out, as if she were too happy to contain herself.

Madison lowered herself slowly to the swivel chair

behind the desk and bit her lower lip viciously as she listened to her mother's excited voice.

Rosalind had remarried. How many husbands did that make now? Her new husband, Roz said, was a very rich older man who showered her with attention and fun and the most exquisite gifts. His grown children *adored* her, and she was now a grandmother.

"Stepgrandmother, of course," Rosalind chirped on. "Of course, no one can believe that I'm old enough to *be* a grandmother—" She paused to laugh at that. "I get so *tired* of everyone constantly remarking that I look too *young* to be a grandma. I'm thinking of simply claiming that I'm their *mommy*. Oh, they're such little dears—three of them now— two precious, *precious* little girls, and one very handsome little boy…"

Madison bowed her head, hurt beyond words. The "little dears" must have had the good fortune to be born beautiful. And God, *three* of them!

"Hastings is eager to meet you, dear," her mother went on, oblivious to the painful silence on Madison's end of the line. "He wants you to come up to Aspen for the weekend. All the children will be here—"

Madison lifted her head as an agony of hope and excitement stormed through her. She'd never *ever* been invited anywhere by her mother. She was acutely aware of how long it had been since she'd even seen Rosalind, because some part of her heart had kept constant track. *Twelve years, three months, a few odd weeks, a handful of days…*

The reminder sent a flash of outrage through her as the truth dawned. The new husband—Hastings?— must have asked more questions than any of Roz's other men had had the sense to. Rosalind probably felt compelled to summon her ugly duckling daughter to her side. Had she somehow found out that Madison had at long last grown into a swan? Maddie knew instantly that she would be expected to parade herself before Roz's new husband and stepfamily to provide her errant mother with some sort of legitimacy and standing with them.

Hastings must be a billionaire.

The cynical thought came naturally to Madison. Her mind darted between the only two options she had, yes or no.

Yes, I'll come today... No, you never wanted me...

Yes to the glimmer of hope? No to the nightmare of pretense. The pain and resentment of a lifetime gave her pride a hard nudge.

"I—I don't know when I can get away," she made herself say.

"Oh dear, we'll only be here until Sunday afternoon!" The coaxing whine Madison had forgotten stirred up more old anger and made her grit her teeth.

"I'll see what I can do, mother. It's so hard to get away *on such short notice.*"

Rosalind was oblivious to the little dig. "Oh, sweetheart, *do* please *try.* Hastings and the children will be so disappointed. I'll be just *devastated* if you can't come up..." She let her voice trail away as if she'd become too emotional to go on.

Someone on Rosalind's end of the line must have been close enough to eavesdrop, which accounted for her Oscar-worthy performance. Madison was suddenly and profoundly sick to her stomach.

"I'll try, Mother," she finally got out.

"Oh, that's my *darling*." Roz's tone switched so quickly to business that she confirmed Madison's suspicion that Roz's pleading just seconds ago was a put-on because she had an audience she wanted to impress.

Roz prattled off a series of directions to the Aspen residence—one of Hastings's five homes in the U.S. Madison didn't bother to write them down. Because they were her mother's words, she'd remember each one as if they'd been carved on her heart with a dull knife.

Clearly confident that Madison would rush to Aspen, Roz ended the brief conversation and hung up.

Madison sat stiffly, dazed, her heart still beating wildly, her stomach still heavy with nausea. The dial tone droned unnoticed for several moments. Finally, she realized she was still pressing the receiver to her ear. She pulled it away and reached over to set it in its cradle. Her hand was shaking violently.

Madison retreated to her room and spent most of Friday pacing. How could Rosalind expect her to fall all over herself to get to Colorado? How could she possibly stay away? The dilemma tied her in knots that seemed to be spiked with thousands of sharp little pins.

She wrestled with the choice, reliving the pain of a lifetime, so wary of opening herself for more that she was literally unable to reach a decision that didn't make her feel ill. By the time she went to bed that night, her head was pounding. She managed to sleep only because she'd worn herself out.

By morning, she convinced herself that she had to

go to Colorado, and called the airlines in San Antonio to book a flight. She soon discovered that the world had conspired to keep her in Texas at least another day.

At first, she was merely annoyed that every flight with connections to Colorado was booked. By midmorning, she was desperate. She'd tried to hire a private flight out of Coulter City, but there were no local pilots available that day, no matter how much money she offered.

Just as she was about to pack and drive to San Antonio to wait on standby or hire a private flight from there, someone from the local airport called her to report that a private pilot had a cancellation and might be available for hire.

Madison rushed upstairs to her room where a maid was hastily packing her clothes.

"*Not* the gray silk, Charlene," Madison said irritably as she snatched the delicate blouse from the garment bag and tossed it aside.

Her nerves were ragged and her tone was sharper than she'd meant, but she ignored the impulse to apologize and paced the room for a few moments while she supervised the packing. It was better not to become too approachable. She didn't want to encourage a personal relationship with any member of her staff. She'd made that mistake in the past and had lived to regret it.

Growing more restless by the moment, she stalked to the bathroom to gather her toiletries for herself— she never trusted a maid with the task of ensuring that every one of her makeup and hair care items were packed.

Finally, she changed her clothes. She selected a red cotton blouse and a pair of khaki bush pants. The low-heeled hiking boots she chose were made of fine-grained leather and lightweight suede. Ankle high, the boots had been chosen more for their chic, outdoorsy look than any true practicality, but they went well with the outfit.

Insecurity made her freshen her makeup, check her polished nails and carefully brush her hair before she scrutinized her image in the mirror. Would her mother even recognize her? Madison turned her head this way and that, searching critically for a glimmer of the homely child she'd been.

Her frequent trips to San Antonio to have her dull blond hair tinted a bright shade just short of platinum was well worth her time and money. She was fanatical about frequent touch-ups and trims. The sleek, collar-length pageboy cut, with the back trimmed slightly shorter than the sides, was simple, elegant and easy to maintain.

Her complexion was clear and the array of skin care products she used kept it flawless. Her delicate features had evened out, her teeth were pearly white and perfectly straight after years of braces, and her slim figure was femininely curved and rigidly maintained by a careful diet. Only the deep blue of her eyes was the same.

Thrilled that the image in the mirror would surely exceed anything her mother could have hoped for, Madison grabbed her handbag and small case, then rushed from the bathroom. Her luggage had already been taken down to the car.

Her heart was pounding with excitement and dread

by the time she settled on the backseat of her Cadillac
and the chauffeur closed the gleaming black door. In
seconds, they were speeding through Coulter City to
the small airport past the edge of town, and Madison
was so nervous that she felt light-headed.

"What do you mean, you can't fly me to Aspen?"

Though the cultured feminine voice wasn't loud or
shrill, it carried from the tarmac on the airstrip side
of the hangar to where Lincoln Coryell had parked
his Jeep. He instantly recognized the cool, acid-edged
tone and felt his good mood sour.

Madison St. John, the reigning queen of Coulter
City, was obviously struggling to comprehend the
word no. A grim smile slanted his lips as he lifted his
gear out of the Jeep and shut the door.

Beautiful, elegant, and filthy rich, Ms. St. John
should have been one of the most sought-after heiresses in Texas. Instead, men avoided the razor-
tongued shrew as diligently as they would a hill of
fire ants. Any man with sense found out right off that
no amount of money was adequate compensation for
the hell he'd have to endure to tangle with her. A
fortune hunter or two had been brave enough to try,
but she had the ability to send any man foolish
enough to get near her running for the nearest mes-
quite patch.

She couldn't be much older than twenty-three, but
she viewed the world with the cynicism and arrogance
of an embittered woman twice her age. Her grandmother, Clara Chandler, had been the same way,
though age and meanness had made her far worse.

Madison hadn't always been the way she was now.

Linc had worked on the ranch her grandmother had owned years ago. He remembered Maddie St. John as an awkward, stick-thin adolescent with straggly hair and a mouth full of hardware. She'd been a sweet kid then, shy, soft-spoken, and polite to everyone.

But that sweet, shy girl had grown up into a spoiled, self-indulgent beauty, so changed that there was no sign that the child she'd been had ever existed.

As he walked past the corner of the hangar to where his small plane was parked, he could finally see Madison with the pilot, Tom Grant.

"You agreed to fly me to Colorado, Mr. Grant," she went on in that imperious tone that worked like sandpaper on the nerves.

"It's a long flight, Miz St. John, and—"

"You want more money." It wasn't a question. Her soft voice had dropped lower and brought to mind the warning growl of a cat.

"No, ma'am," Tom said, shaking his head as if he were anxious to correct her impression. "Just that the wife decided she hadn't seen much of me this week and won't stand to have me gone most of the weekend after those other folks canceled. Said she wanted me home."

"How *sweet.*" Madison's soft remark was poisonous, and Tom shifted nervously from one foot to the other. Linc could imagine the look she was giving the man, though he could only see her profile as he passed several feet away from where they stood.

Tom caught sight of him then and gave a quick wave to get his attention. "Linc Coryell's right over there, Miz St. John. Heard he was flyin' to Aspen— hey, Linc!"

Madison turned to look in the direction Tom Grant indicated. The pilot broke into a trot and rushed to intercept Lincoln Coryell. As she watched, Tom jerked a thumb in her direction, said something too low for her to hear, then turned to hurry toward the airstrip office.

Incensed that the pilot had distracted her and neatly escaped, she stiffened when she felt Linc level his gaze on her. He was wearing a pair of mirrored sunglasses. The shade of his black Stetson would have made it impossible to read the expression in his dark eyes from this distance, but the sunglasses projected an aloofness that made him appear unapproachable.

She saw his mouth tighten before he glanced away and walked on. Unwilling to let this opportunity go by, she started after him. Her boots thumped smartly on the concrete as she tried to catch up.

Though she had an aversion to men like Lincoln Coryell—blunt, macho and uncivilized—she could endure a few hours of his presence if he could get her to Aspen. Instinct rather than past experience told her he was one of the few men in this part of Texas who was completely unimpressed by either her name or her wealth.

But then, Lincoln Coryell wasn't a man to show deference to many. He was too hard and rough-edged and rich to be intimidated, and though the former cowboy was probably more wealthy than she was, his lack of education—she'd heard he hadn't finished high school—and his ranch hand background excluded him from being a close member of the small society of elites in and around Coulter City.

She suspected a man like him could never be

bought or finessed, and the only intimidation that would come into play with him was the strange intimidation *she* felt suddenly.

She pasted a faint smile on her face to signal the friendliness she needed to project, but the necessity of doing so made her grit her teeth. She could find another flight, but probably not until tomorrow. It was only because tomorrow might be too late that she even considered using charm.

"Mr. Coryell?" she said as she finally caught up with him, "I understand you're flying to Colorado."

Those mirrored sunglasses flashed toward her briefly as they walked along. She forced herself to smile a bit wider while he was looking down at her, but the effort felt more like an awkward twitch. The sunglasses flashed again with a dismissive turn of his head.

Nettled, she walked faster to keep up with his long stride. "I'm more than willing to pay," she added, struggling to keep her voice reasonable and pleasant. She felt the snub when he didn't respond. Surprise made her slow her steps. When he continued on, she hesitated, then hurried after him, appalled by the indignity of having to pursue him.

"I need to get to Colorado by evening, Mr. Coryell," she called, her frustration mounting higher as she was forced to practically chase the man. Feeling her cheeks heat with embarrassment, she sent a swift glance toward the office and hangar to see if anyone was watching.

In the next moment, she crashed into Linc's back. He'd slowed when she wasn't looking and she'd blundered into him. She gasped and jumped back as if she'd been burned.

And she had been. The heat of his big body and his sun-warmed clothes had scorched her somehow and it was all she could do not to check herself for damage. But he'd turned toward her and his handsome mouth was set in a no-nonsense line that warned her he was irritated.

Knowing she had to be polite if she had any hope of persuading him to fly her to Colorado, she forced another smile that felt as twitchy and unnatural as the other one had. "Pardon me, Mr. Coryell. I didn't expect you to slow down so…abruptly."

Her apology automatically implied that *he* was in the wrong for stopping, which he was. But he didn't take blame well. She could tell by the hardening of his firm jaw.

Compelled to recover from her faux pas, she was forced to add, "I wasn't watching where I was going for a moment." She hesitated, giving herself a moment to conceal her aversion to apologizing twice. "Pardon me."

She hadn't realized how tall and broad-shouldered Lincoln Coryell was until she was standing two feet in front of him. The top of her head barely came to his shoulder. The mirrored lenses of his sunglasses were aimed down at her, and seeing twin reflections of herself made her feel even smaller.

That she also felt more fragile and feminine than she'd ever felt in her life was a small shock. But then, she'd just run into his hard body, and the impression of his solid masculinity was still quaking through her.

He didn't speak, just stared down at her from his

superior height as if neither of her apologies had been enough. Frustrated by his taciturn manner and uncertain how to deal effectively with him, she took advantage of his undivided attention.

"I have a very serious reason to get to Colorado—to Aspen—by tonight, Mr. Coryell." Stung when he still didn't respond, she gritted her teeth and made herself go on. "It's not quite life or death, but close. I'm willing to pay you for your time and inconvenience—double the fare the other pilot asked."

Finally, he reacted. But the cynical slant of his handsome mouth was insultingly superior. *No one* looked down their nose at Madison St. John, yet the impression she had that Lincoln Coryell was doing just that jolted her.

"I don't hire out, Miz St. John." With that, he turned and walked away.

Maddie's frustration spiked so high that she felt dizzy with it. She had to get to Colorado. Though she could drive to San Antonio and try to catch a flight from there, she had no guarantee of success. Lincoln Coryell was flying to Colorado *now*. Besides, she'd compromised her dignity too far with him to take no for an answer. His resistance to her—though she was straining to be pleasant to him—was offensive. *Demeaning*.

The picture that flashed in her mind—of her mother's reaction when she finally set eyes on the ugly duckling daughter who'd grown into a swan—sharpened her determination.

Perhaps Roz would regret the years of neglect. A secret part of Madison's heart hoped her mother would be sorry for abandoning her, but without

Lincoln Coryell's help, it might never happen. If she didn't get to Colorado today or by afternoon tomorrow, God only knew when—or if—her mother would contact her again.

She started after him, forced to set an unladylike pace to catch up.

"Mr. Coryell!" The hint of ire that simmered beneath her soft tone had worked with scores of others. In the end, she knew of only one sure way to assert her will over his and make him take her to Colorado. "As I said, it's very important that I get to Aspen by tonight," she insisted as she caught up and fell into step beside him.

Linc's long strides didn't alter. "So you said," he drawled. "Not quite life or death, but close," he quoted as they reached his small plane. He stopped and tossed his duffel bag out of the way near the tail of the aircraft, then turned toward her. The mirrored sunglasses flashed down at her and again framed her image.

"But not close enough to life or death for you to consider using a word as ordinary and humbling as the word *please.*"

Linc watched Maddie's lips part, saw the spasm of shock in her eyes that blanked the arrogance from her stiff expression. Clearly, words like "please" and maybe even "thank you" weren't a regular part of her vocabulary.

He stared down at her frozen expression, a little surprised at himself for giving her even a small chance to wreck what had started out to be a good day.

On the other hand, there was something challenging about a gorgeous, sharp-tongued shrew who intimidated the hell out of most men. Normally, he wanted no part of a female as self-centered and high-maintenance as Maddie St. John. Her flawless appearance hinted at excessive vanity, and it was an easy bet that she'd never warmed enough to any man to tolerate getting a little disheveled.

What would it take to get a woman like her to mellow? Was her legendary bitchiness born of meanness, or had she spoiled and overindulged herself on her inheritance? Was there any real passion behind her cool, blond beauty, or was she an ice cube through and through?

Her father and mother had abandoned her to a grandmother who'd bullied her mercilessly. Linc knew she hadn't had an easy life. He hadn't either, but he'd overcome it and made several fortunes by seeing the potential in losing propositions and by taking big risks.

And for all her stunning beauty and wealth, Madison St. John was a losing proposition. Maybe there wasn't anything about her worth having, but if there was, it might be entertaining to find it. The only thing he'd truly risk was a few hours cooped up with her in a small plane.

Still, he'd leave her right there on the tarmac if she couldn't lower her haughty attitude far enough to frame a proper request that included the word "please." She'd had so much trouble with "pardon me" that "please" might be more than she could handle.

He waited as the seconds stretched, watched as the flush in her cheeks darkened and rose higher. Just when he was about to grab his gear and stow it in the plane, her gaze wavered and fell from his.

He saw her chin lift slightly in defiance of the small defeat. She didn't look him in the eye; probably afraid she'd see a hint of triumph. If the situation were reversed and she'd been the one who'd got the upper hand, it was a sure bet he would have seen triumph in hers.

"It's very important that I get to Aspen by tonight, Mr. Coryell." The careful words and her neutral tone were obviously straining her. "Would...would you please consider allowing me to fly to Colorado with you?"

The way she'd looked when she said the words— as if she'd just been forced to consent to the most hideous, immoral act in the history of man—startled a chuckle out of him.

Those blue, blue eyes leaped to make the connection with his, and he saw the conflagration that burst up in their vivid depths. She was furious, but to her credit, she didn't turn it loose on him. Instead, she pressed her lips together so tightly that they were little more than a colorless seam.

"Go get your luggage and haul it over by mine while I do my preflight."

The new flash of outrage in her eyes told him the order had heaped a new indignity on her injured pride. He hadn't used the word "please" himself, but he'd meant to leave it out. He could tell she knew it.

Her face flushed with the temper they both knew she didn't dare vent on him, Madison turned and stalked back to the collection of monogrammed luggage near the hangar. Linc spared a few moments to watch her go, admiring the faint sway of hips that her rigid stride didn't quite repress.

# CHAPTER TWO

MADISON SAT STIFFLY beside him, her posture so straight that it should have snapped her spine. Her hauteur amused him. Madison St. John was too full of herself; money had ruined the sweet kid she'd been. She was living proof that it wasn't healthy to get everything you wanted. A body had to have something meaningful to look forward to, some reason to dream.

He thought again about how much she'd changed. Madison and her cousin, Caitlin Bodine, had been close once. But as far as he knew, they hadn't spoken to each other for years. It was no secret that Madison blamed Caitlin for the death of the boy she'd been in love with in high school.

Beau Duvall had been a rounder, spoiled by his mother and stepfather, and destined for trouble, but shy, plain little Maddie had been crazy about him. When Beau was killed, she'd been devastated and, like everyone else, she'd blamed Caitlin.

It was only in the past few months, after Caitlin had returned to Texas, that the whole truth about Beau's death had been made public. Caitlin had not only been accepted back into everyone's good graces, she'd married Beau Duvall's older brother, Reno. Madison was the only person who couldn't accept what had really happened when Beau was killed.

Her reason for being the only holdout was probably

nothing he'd ever know. He'd rarely had personal contact with her. The moment they got to Colorado and went their separate ways, he wouldn't have cause to have contact with her again. Though they both lived in the same part of Texas and were both wealthy, their lifestyles were too different for anything more than a distant acquaintance.

Madison couldn't relax. Her choler had faded, displaced by the agonizing fear she had of small planes. Because she confided in no one these days, no one would ever guess the magnitude of what she was willing to go through to see her mother.

The large Cessna seemed so cramped and fragile. It bumped and wallowed over every little pocket of air. The constant motion made her queasy, and the longer they flew, the heavier the queasiness became. Hours into the flight, she was so nauseous that she could barely sit upright. She'd wilted back against the seat, so miserable she was shaking.

"Your face is a pretty shade of green, Miz St. John."

Linc's calm observation gave her a vicious start.

"You need a bucket?"

The crude question put a sickening image in her mind. Grappling for the distraction of sarcasm, she said through gritted teeth, "Your lap should do well enough, Mr. Coryell."

The sudden dip of the plane almost pushed her queasy stomach over the edge. She squeezed her eyes closed and panted sickly as the plane began to descend. She was aware of Linc reaching for the radio mike, but she couldn't follow what he said into it.

Her attention had fixed on the low, calm sound of his voice. The unexpected comfort of his masculine drawl slid along her ragged nerves and steadied them somehow. The strange reaction set off a small shock wave that made her turn her head weakly against the seat back to look at him.

Lincoln Coryell was handsome, ruggedly so. His broad-shouldered, six-foot-four frame seemed to fill the cabin of the small plane, making it seem even more crowded. His arm and side were inches away, but she felt the heat of him from where she sat. Pleasant heat. Male heat.

The pang of guilt she felt surprised her until she let herself acknowledge its source.

Beau Duvall. She'd loved Beau deeply. She still loved him. He'd been handsome, so beautifully handsome. Love of life had blazed so painfully bright in his blue eyes, in his tanned face, in everything he said and did and wanted in life. He'd been so much fun, teasing, irreverent and daring.

Maddie had been so repressed, so unloved, so unlovely back then that when such a handsome, vitally alive and exciting young man had paid the slightest attention to her, she'd fallen wildly and hopelessly in love, dismally aware that handsome Beau Duvall could never love her.

But then he *had*. The miracle of it still awed her, still gave her hungry heart some vital bit of sustenance, though Beau was long dead now. Beau's affection for her had been like a fairy tale come true. He'd made her feel wanted, special; he'd made her feel beautiful, somehow bringing about her astonishing transformation from duckling to swan...

Linc turned his head to look at her. Though she was remembering Beau, she'd been staring at Linc. He said something and her blurry gaze fell to his lips. They were so well-defined, with a masculine sort of ruthlessness that made her heart flutter lightly despite her misery.

Linc's face was tanned and harshly chiseled, but brutally attractive in the way of rugged Western men who spent their days in the elements working with dangerous animals.

Dangerous. Yes, she realized, her mind still fuzzy. Dangerous was the word for the way Lincoln Coryell looked. Tough was also part of the package, but he was one hundred percent domineering Texas male, from the crown of his Stetson to the underslung heels of his Western boots.

Nothing at all like the much less harsh, far more gentle and sweet Beau. Never like Beau.

So why this peculiar stirring with Linc, why this sudden fascination with a man too hard-edged and blatantly male for her refined tastes?

Madison turned her head so she wouldn't have to look at him. She felt so horribly ill. Surely these wild impressions and startling reactions were part of being in such utter physical misery.

The abrupt jolt of the small plane setting down made her jerk with surprise. Relief flooded her as she realized they'd landed, and Linc was taxiing off the runway to the tarmac next to a hangar. Her head was still swimming after he brought the plane to a halt and switched off the engine. She was so nauseous that she didn't dare move. Her eyelids sagged closed as she waited for her stomach to settle.

"Did you eat something today?"

The gruff question sent a sting of irritation across her jittery nerves. The nausea surged up for a moment before it began to recede.

Her soft, "Of course," was a lie. Admitting that she'd been too nervous to eat would reveal a weakness to him that she considered far worse than being airsick.

"You can get a sandwich at the café over there. I'll meet you when the plane's refueled."

Maddie didn't respond until he touched her arm. The earthquake he set off shook her. She roused herself and sat up straighter.

"Come on, Princess. Let's get you outta here."

The gruff words were her only warning before she found herself forcibly ejected from her seat. Panicked, she grabbed her handbag and tried to get out of the plane under her own power. But her arms and legs were clumsy, and her head was whirling.

Linc took over as if she weighed no more than an awkward piece of luggage. He was like some gigantic warm wave, sweeping her small body along ahead of his until he set her on her feet behind the plane's wing.

The bones in her legs were as substantial as cooked noodles, and she swayed against him, clinging to his lean waist as best she could while she tried to recover her strength. The feel of Linc's hard, well-defined masculinity sobered her, but a new kind of weakness spread through her and slowed her recovery.

"Should I get out the smelling salts...or are you makin' a pass at me?"

It took a moment for Linc's drawled words to penetrate.

*Or are you makin' a pass at me?* The idea appalled her. It was amazing how suddenly her legs steadied and she was able to push him away.

"God forbid." The caustic words slipped out before she considered how sharply they might land on a male ego. Most male egos were pathetically fragile. Normally, she didn't care whether she trampled one or not, but she needed Linc's goodwill.

Her gaze shot up to gauge his reaction, but his sunglasses blocked the sight. What she could see of his face indicated total immunity to the jab.

*Of course.* A man who'd achieved as much wealth and power as Lincoln Coryell couldn't have a fragile ego. Pride maybe. *Excessive* pride. But there was nothing fragile about the tower of masculinity before her.

"Order me some coffee while you're at it," he said, then turned and walked toward the hangar without a backward glance.

Madison managed to eat a good portion of the salad and dry toast she'd ordered before Linc joined her at the café. After little more than an hour on the ground, they were taking off. Madison felt worlds better, but she couldn't get over her nervousness in the small plane. Though she didn't feel much safer in an airliner, small planes always gave her the sensation of hurtling through space in a soda can.

She and Linc didn't speak, and eventually she dozed as the stress of the day caught up with her and the drone of the engine lulled her to sleep.

It was the odd sound of the engine that woke her later. At first, she thought they were landing. But the staccato sound of an engine failing and the irregular vibration that shook the plane registered. Terror brought her fully awake. She jerked her head in Linc's direction.

"What's wrong?" Linc's sunglasses were off and his lean jaw was clenched so hard that she knew the answer before he spoke.

"Tighten that seat belt and hang on."

The grim order made her face forward to see out the windshield. Mountains. They were over the Rockies. The deep, heavy green of forest that mantled everything below the highest peaks and seemed to fill every valley between was breathtaking. The realization that they were about to fall into all those trees— and would probably be killed in a fiery crash—was so vivid suddenly that she couldn't breathe. Every wild beat of her heart thundered in her ears as she watched the mountains and all that green come closer and closer.

Her body went so rigid with tension that she was in literal pain. Terror left her dry-mouthed and mute. But when the plane suddenly lurched to the left, her stomach lurched with it and startled a gurgling shriek out of her.

Her shock-rounded eyes flew to Linc and she saw him grappling with the controls. It took her a moment to register the fact that he'd turned the plane on purpose. Though it was out of control, he'd managed to force it to do something.

"What are you *doing?*" Her demand didn't convey any of her insight, but it was as close as she dared to the question she really wanted to have answered: *Are we going to die?*

A cowardice she'd never suspected of herself gripped her insides. They were about to die and she wasn't ready!

The plane dipped crazily and suddenly she could see the treetops loom so close she felt as if she could put out her hand and touch them. She could see the individual leaves on the branches and instinctively pressed her feet against the floor in an irrational attempt to push herself higher.

"Cover your face!"

Madison was too frozen to move. The last thing she glimpsed before the nose of the plane came up and blocked her view was a space of open meadow.

And then the terrible sound of treetops scraping metal filled the plane. She leaned forward and covered her face with her arms. She must have fainted then because she never felt the crash.

Linc wiped impatiently at the trickle of sweat that slid down between his eyebrows, not surprised that his fingers came away bloody. His head hurt like hell, but he was alive. He wasn't sure how long he'd been unconscious, but it couldn't have been long. The sun—what he could tell about its position with trees blocking its light—hadn't moved too far. But he'd been out long enough that the smell of leaking fuel was strong.

He glanced over at his passenger. Maddie finally looked disheveled. Her chin rested on her chest, and she looked as limp as a rag doll. She didn't seem to have a mark on her, so he reached over to touch her arm and give her a small shake. She stirred then, lifted her head, and let out a small moan.

Madison felt as if every joint in her body had been dislocated. Consciousness ebbed back and with it the memory of falling through the trees. She jerked fully awake and glanced around wildly. Outside the missing windows of the cockpit, tree trunks and branches were everywhere. The tip of a branch had speared through a window space far enough that it was only six inches from her face.

"You all right?" The brusque question startled her, but when she turned her head to look over at Linc, her neck was stiff with pain. The terror and disorientation she felt eased at the comforting sight of him.

He was no longer wearing his Stetson. A cut near his hairline glistened with blood, but other than the cut, he looked as rugged and domineering as ever. His skin was a little gray beneath his tan, but he looked wonderfully, gloriously unharmed.

He gave her arm a small shake that made her aware he was speaking to her. "Are you all right?"

The question sounded a little kinder this time, and for some reason, her eyes began to smart with tears. Appalled, she forced them back and focused on mentally checking herself for injuries. Other than a stiff neck and a body that ached everywhere, she felt remarkably unharmed.

The realization that she was alive sent a gust of pure euphoria through her. "I seem to be...fine."

Linc didn't look as euphoric as she felt. In fact, his expression was so grim that she felt a surge of anxiety.

"Then we'd better get out. Carefully," he added, "since we've got a fuel leak."

Madison smelled it now, and it was strong. She automatically reached for her handbag, then had to rummage on the floor for it. Thankfully, it had been securely zipped so its contents hadn't been scattered.

Linc bustled her out of the plane as quickly and forcefully as he had at the airport, but they had to fight their way through the broken branches and underbrush that jammed the space around the right wing.

Once they were on the ground, Madison stumbled through the brush, using her handbag to cover her face until they were past the tail of the plane. The meadow she'd glimpsed before the crash was just a few feet away.

Linc had obviously not had enough room to land before he ran out of clearing and smashed into the trees. When Madison turned and saw that the nose and body of the plane had speared neatly into a narrow gap between the tree trunks, she couldn't help being impressed with his aim.

But because the plane had gone into the trees, the crash wouldn't be easy to spot from the sky. It dawned on her that the hidden crash made it next to impossible for a quick rescue. Linc's next words confirmed it.

"I'll get as much gear and luggage as I can. When I throw it out, drag it to the clearing."

Madison glanced toward the meadow, then back at the plane. The smell of fuel was still strong. "W-will it blow up?"

Linc ignored her question and started toward the

wreck. She seized his arm and held him back, terrified of an explosion.

"We need what's in the plane, if we can get it."

Madison let go of his arm. Of course they needed what was in the plane. The clothing she'd brought, her makeup and toiletries, were necessities. But not if the plane was about to explode.

She was terrified again, this time for Linc. If the plane blew up, he'd be killed or seriously injured, and they were too far from help. All she'd seen from the air had been miles of trees and mountains. Anxious for Linc's safety, Madison followed, but hovered a safe distance from the wreck.

The first things Linc tossed her way must have been his. A packaged blanket, a rope, a bundled piece of plastic, and his duffel bag. Finally, he got to her luggage and hefted out her small suitcase to send it tumbling toward her. She winced when it hit the ground sharply. Panicked, she grabbed it and gave it a careful shake. The sound of small bottles clacking against one another made her hurry through the brush to the clearing to check the fragile contents.

The catch had jammed and she crouched down beside Linc's things to set her case on the ground and force it open. She was so absorbed in the task and so worried that the contents had been damaged, that she forgot to go back to the plane to help with the rest of her luggage.

"Thanks much, Princess."

The sound of the suitcase and garment bag hitting the ground next to her made her jump. Madison frowned at the luggage he'd dropped, then jerked her head up to glare at him. He'd located his Stetson and it cast an appealing shadow over his handsome face.

"How dare you throw my belongings around?"

One corner of his handsome mouth quirked. "Didn't exactly throw them. Unless you'd like me to demonstrate what that would look like, so you can tell the difference."

Something about the way his dark eyes shifted to her large suitcase made her reach toward it protectively.

But Linc stepped over it to get to his duffel bag. Madison watched him mistrustfully until he unzipped the bag before she went back to the stubborn catch on her small case.

"Go through your things and pick out a few essentials," he told her as he sorted through his bag, discarding one thing after another.

Madison ignored the order. He might have packed things he didn't consider essential, but she hadn't. She needed everything she'd brought.

Especially the contents of the small case. The catch remained stubbornly closed. She reached for her handbag to find something she could use to pry it open. The Cadillac key on her key ring was sturdier than her metal fingernail file, so she used it. But the key was too thick for the thin crack of the case.

"Get busy with that luggage."

Linc's terse words brought her head up. He was hunkered down, balancing himself on the balls of his booted feet with a forearm resting on a bowed thigh. He'd finished going through his duffel bag and was watching her expectantly. She could see he'd packed the roll of plastic and the rope. The blanket must have been packed in the deeper part of the bag. A pile of clothing sat on the ground next to him.

"I *am* busy with my luggage," she shot back irritably. "And you *did* throw this case. You damaged the catch."

"Hand it here and start on the rest of your things."

Maddie looked over at him a moment, reluctant. Did she really trust him with it? What if he managed to open the latch and saw the contents—*looked through* the contents? Her makeup and toiletries—her feminine hygiene products—were things she considered too personal for male eyes. Certainly too personal for Lincoln Coryell's eyes.

Eyes that were so brown they were almost black, she noticed, and so intense that they seemed to miss nothing. She suddenly had the feeling that they were probing deep into her brain, as if he could read her next thought before she knew it herself.

No one had ever looked at her like that; she'd never have allowed it. She wouldn't have allowed Linc to do so now except she couldn't seem to look away. She couldn't seem to keep from noticing how attractive his dark eyes were, and how frightening and wonderful it was to feel the odd power of them stroking so deep, so—

The small case slid from her fingers, startling her. She grabbed for it reflexively, but wasn't quick enough to snatch it. A tug of war would have been undignified, so she pulled back and clenched her fists.

"Sort through that luggage." The order was low, but this time, it carried a burr of steel that chafed her pride. "Pick the essentials."

Her firm, "Everything I packed is essential,"

brought his dark gaze homing in on hers like an arrow on a target.

"Humor me, Princess. I'm having a bad day."

The harsh set of his mouth was surprisingly intimidating. And effective. Madison hesitated a moment before reaching for the suitcase. When she did, those dark eyes fell away to focus on the small case.

Madison opened the large suitcase, gave everything a token perusal, then snapped it shut. She went through the garment bag just as swiftly.

"Valium?"

The gruff question got her attention and Madison glanced Linc's way. He'd got the small case open and she automatically reached for it before the grim look on his face registered. He was holding a prescription bottle between two callused fingers.

"You addicted to these things?" His obvious disapproval made her give a quick, "Of course not." He ignored her outstretched hand.

"How often do you take them?"

She leaned forward to claim the bottle from him, but he closed his hand and held it just out of reach.

"How often?" The no-nonsense look he was giving her warned he meant business.

Madison's temper shot high and hot. "None of your business. Give them to me."

Instead, he glanced down at the bottle to read the label. "Looks like a big dose for a beginner."

She felt her face flush. "Are you suggesting I'm an addict?"

He leveled a hard look on her and studied her face a moment. "What's a woman like you got to be nervous about?"

The low question hit her like a slap. Linc Coryell had not only gone over the line, he'd managed to strike deep into painful places. The emotion that surged up caught her by surprise and her eyes were suddenly stinging.

"You don't know what you're talking about," she shot back, dismayed that her voice was choked. And that made her angry. "Give me the bottle."

Linc slipped it into his shirt pocket and buttoned the pocket flap. The action sent her temper skyrocketing.

*"How dare you?"* Her voice shook with outrage.

"You keep asking that, Miz Maddie," he said calmly, his gaze unwavering. "I dare a lot, and I'll dare a damn sight more in the next few days. But I'd rather walk out of here with a neurotic sissy on my hands than a neurotic *stoned* sissy." He nodded in the direction of her luggage. "Now let's get that out of the way."

The quick shift of subject and his smooth move to reach for the large suitcase caught her off guard.

He had it open in a moment and began to sort through everything. The sight of his big hands rifling carelessly through her personal belongings offended her.

"I need everything there," she repeated, then reached over to close the lid of the suitcase. Before she could, Linc seized her wrist. Her gaze flew to his.

"Look around, Maddie."

The solemn order sent a spear of terror through her that made her forget her luggage. The utter grimness on Linc's face was unmistakable. A picture of dense green forest and high mountains flashed in her mind.

But the endless forest she'd glimpsed from the sky would look even more awesome and terrible from the ground. The weird sensation she had—that the wilderness was closing in around them—sent her terror bounding higher. In spite of Linc's order, she couldn't look around, couldn't make herself.

# CHAPTER THREE

LINC SAW THE TERROR in her eyes. He could also see that she was in shock. Madison St. John might be vain and obsessed with her looks, but she wasn't stupid. She had at least enough common sense to know they couldn't carry everything out of the mountains with them. Her fixation on her luggage was a denial of what lay ahead for them both: a long and probably dangerous hike through the wilderness. And certainly the worst hardship imaginable for a pampered little aristocrat like her.

He felt the weight of the valium bottle in his pocket. If she couldn't cope with life's little jiggles without sedation, she'd never get through this. Instinct warned him not to coddle her. If he did, she'd go to pieces. If he could tap into her legendary temper and distract her, they'd both be better off.

He released her. He ignored the way she rubbed the wrist he'd touched, almost as if she was trying to soothe away pain. There shouldn't have been any pain for her to soothe.

He hesitated a moment more to study her pale face. She wasn't looking at him now; she was staring to the left of the suitcase into the grass. Her slim, perfectly manicured fingers still circled her wrist, but the soothing motion she made was an absent one. Clearly, her mind was on other things—and from the stark look of vulnerability about her—she was about to fall apart.

Linc glanced into the suitcase. He spied a small, neatly folded stack of frilly panties and grabbed them. They were the first things he sent sailing into the grass, making sure they landed in the exact spot her eyes were focused on. A flimsy scrap of bra followed before he got down to business with the contents of her suitcase and silently counted the seconds.

Two...three...

"How *dare* you?"

She'd used that low cat growl again. He pretended to ignore her as he lifted out a sky-blue satin robe and stripped the tie belt from its loops. He discarded the robe beside the suitcase, but tossed the belt toward the duffel bag. He added two rolls of thick white socks to the satin belt, and a stack of packaged panty hose. Next, a fold of netting got his attention and he pulled it out. It was a bag, probably for dirty clothes, and it was a good size. He gripped the netting in his hands and gave it a stout yank to test its strength before he tossed it to the pile on top of the duffel bag.

Madison looked on, appalled at his rough treatment of her belongings. It was clear that he only meant to select a few odds and ends from her suitcase before he forced her to leave everything else behind. She clutched the wad of panties and bra to herself. My God she couldn't go anywhere without clean underwear! The fact that he'd thrown her most intimate apparel into the grass with bugs and chiggers infuriated her.

Wary of him because he was so rough with her things, Madison cautiously reached for the satin robe and bundled her underwear in it. She retrieved the net bag from the top of his duffel and stuffed the rolled robe into it.

Linc got out her shoebag next and rummaged through it, selecting the athletic shoes she'd had packed. He tossed them in her direction and they fell to the ground at her feet.

"Put those on and take the laces out of the boots you're wearing."

Madison stared down at the shoes, then at the light-weight boots. "These are hiking boots," she said, struggling to keep her voice steady while she defied the order. She'd accidentally glimpsed the dense wall of trees on the other side of the high meadow. The sensation of wilderness creeping closer was strong again. Arguing with Linc was the only thing she could think of to distract herself from mindless terror.

"Fakes," he said bluntly. "The leather's like paper compared to the other pair."

Madison stared down at the white athletic shoes, her thoughts racing. The very fact that he'd ordered her to switch her faux hiking boots for sturdy athletic shoes suggested that he anticipated an ordeal far more lengthy and arduous than a short hike in the woods. And he was right about the boots. The leather was flimsy compared to the Nikes.

"Change the damned shoes, Princess. We've only got so much daylight."

The terse order brought her eyes to his face, but he wasn't looking at her. He grabbed the things he'd discarded and crammed them back into her suitcase before he closed the lid and pressed down on the latches. Then he unzipped her garment bag to paw through the carefully pressed clothing in there. He added another belt to the pile, then two crisply pressed pairs of jeans and two cotton blouses.

Madison quickly grabbed the jeans and blouses and packed them into the net bag. Thank goodness she wouldn't have to fight with him about extra clothes. At least she'd have something clean to wear later.

*Later.*

How much later? How many hours would it take to walk back to civilization?

Her next thought—that she might not get to Aspen in time to catch her mother—set off an explosion of panic.

"How long will it take to get to Aspen?"

Linc looked at her then, his mouth shifting into a sarcastic slant as he harshly surveyed her from head to foot. "The way you're movin', about a month." He swiftly zipped the garment bag and shoved it toward the suitcase before he stood.

Madison couldn't seem to move as the implication of not getting to Aspen in time began to impact her. If she embarrassed her mother with her new husband by not showing up, she'd never hear from Roz again. She'd forever lose the chance to be close to her. Roz would never know she'd outgrown her homeliness. She'd never know a moment's sorrow for giving up on her only child and abandoning her.

"Get busy, sweetheart."

The order snapped her out of her thoughts. The way he'd said the word "sweetheart" was no endearment. She hated the male condescension in his low drawl. And she *loathed* the pet name, "Princess".

Her gaze narrowed with sudden inspiration.

"Right away...*Ace,*" she answered, the stiff stretch of lips she gave him hinting at an acid smile. She had the satisfaction of seeing a glint of reaction in his dark eyes, and let her lips stretch a fraction wider to signal how much she savored the little dig.

Feeling she'd avenged herself in some small way, she stepped over to sit on her large suitcase to change her shoes. By the time she'd worked the laces from the hiking boots, Linc had packed everything but her net bag of clothing into his duffel bag.

Having second thoughts about the hiking boots—she hated being limited to one pair of shoes—she slipped them into the net bag.

And then Linc was walking away from her toward the trees on the other side of the meadow, his long stride rapidly putting distance between them.

In her rush to gather her purse and the net bag to catch up with him, Madison almost missed getting the small case that held her cosmetics and toiletries. She slung her purse strap over one shoulder, the cord of the net bag over the other, then picked up the small case to hurry after Linc.

She'd gone half a dozen steps before she managed to trip on a thick tuft of meadow grass and fall flat.

Linc set a pace he knew was brutal for Madison. He wasn't doing it to be cruel, but to hurry her along so fast that she'd pay more attention to keeping up with him than on the predicament they were in.

And he knew enough about her poison-pill personality to guess that her little "Ace" dig was the prelude to a major tirade on the subject of the crash. She

had the potential to harangue him every step of the
way if he gave her an opportunity.

He assumed the fastest course out of the mountains
was to keep walking downhill. They needed to find a
stream and a safe place to camp before dark. Once
the sun dropped behind the western peaks they'd lose
the light. Her Highness wouldn't take that well at all.

At least they'd be able to start a fire. He had
matches and a lighter, but they'd need water. They
could miss a few meals, but they could only go so
long without water. Finding a stream might also mean
that they could catch some fish and solve the problem
of food.

He glanced over his shoulder at Madison. She was
still carrying that damned little suitcase. She'd criss-
crossed her purse strap and the cord from the net bag
over her chest to free her hands, but she carried the
little suitcase as if it contained a bottle of nitroglyc-
erin.

Maybe it did. It held enough cosmetics and groom-
ing items to rival a makeup counter, as well as a small
drugstore of over-the-counter medications. He'd seen
women's toiletries and personal care collections before, but Maddie's put them all to shame. Who had
time to use everything she carried with her?

And for what? Madison St. John was a natural
beauty. She should have been able to wash her face,
comb her hair and walk out of her mansion looking
like a million bucks. Instead, she painted over her
natural good looks as if she were trying to smuggle
a troll out of the house.

He hadn't made a fuss about her bringing the small
case because he'd recognized that at least a few of

the things in her collection might come in handy if they couldn't find their way to civilization soon. He hoped for a ranger's station, a private cabin or a hunting lodge with a telephone, but the chance of that was slim at best. He couldn't guess at how many square miles of wilderness lay around them. Finding anyone else in so vast a place by accident would be impossible.

Besides, they'd used up a huge piece of luck when they'd survived the plane crash. It would be foolish to count on finding more.

Madison was exhausted and miserable, and her feet felt as if they'd been rubbed raw. The athletic shoes were new and turned out to be less than a perfect fit. It didn't matter that they'd been walking downhill for what must have been hours. There was no real path, and the course Linc chose was cluttered with obstacles. A tree root here, a fallen branch there, a clump of brush or a drop-off almost every other step. Sometimes the direction he led was so steep that she often fell on her backside and slid to the bottom.

She was now a sweaty, filthy mess, and she was so thirsty her tongue stuck to her teeth. Linc's long legs made the going easy for him, but she barely managed to keep up. He stayed so far ahead of her that conversation was impossible even if she hadn't been so out of breath.

She'd lost her fear of the wilderness closing in on her. Now that she'd become closely acquainted with the rough terrain—and carried so much of it on her person—resentment and rising anger were her predominant emotions.

What had gone wrong with the plane? Why hadn't Linc used the radio to call for help? Couldn't they have stayed near the plane and started a signal fire or something? Surely there was a more sane alternative than tramping over half the Rocky Mountains.

Linc was rushing them along on purpose, probably to torment her. He knew she was at a greater physical disadvantage than he was, and he clearly meant to use it against her. She knew he didn't like her.

But, so what? No one else did, so she wasn't about to perish of a broken heart. She didn't like him at all. If anything, this hideous little adventure would neutralize the crazy attraction she felt toward him. She doubted very much if his touch would ever again set off the amazing thrill of electricity it had earlier when he'd grabbed her wrist. The very female reaction she'd had when she'd bumped into his big solid body at the airport would likely never happen again either, now that she'd had such a large dose of his chauvinistic, domineering personality and rough, ill-mannered ways.

And she was heartily tired of him racing so far ahead of her in some macho demonstration of male superiority. It was time to assert her own version of machismo.

The decision gave her aching legs a fresh burst of strength and she doggedly closed the distance between them. She was so breathless with the effort in the high elevation that she was light-headed by the time she caught up with him.

Madison managed to grab the back of his shirt the precise second that a field of strange dark spots surged into her vision.

And then the universe—Linc's blue shirt, those damnable trees, everything—winked out.

She was dreaming of rain. It drizzled onto her face in wet, deliciously cool drops. The ugly nightmare she'd been having about plane crashes and mountains and trees receded beneath the refreshing chill of water on her skin.

Madison forced her eyes open to look at the delightfully gentle rain. Lincoln Coryell's stern, handsome features swam into such clear focus that she gasped. The nightmare came roaring back.

Linc held a wadded washcloth from her small case in his big hand. She could feel his arm behind her neck and shoulders supporting her head. His long fingers flexed, squeezing a few more drops of water from the cloth, though he could plainly see that she was awake.

Irritated, she knocked his hand away and abruptly sat up. A wave of dizziness made her jerk up a hand to her forehead, but the sudden movement was awkward and distressingly uncoordinated. Linc's hard fingers gripped her shoulder to keep her upright.

"Go slow, Princess. It's probably the altitude."

"Stop calling me that." Her irritable tone was spoiled by an odd breathlessness as she struggled against the dizziness. Her mouth was dust dry.

Her fuzzy brain finally registered the wet washcloth and she dropped her hand to focus anxiously on Linc's face. "Water—you had water."

Linc turned his head and nodded to a spot somewhere behind her. "Leftover rainwater in a shallow puddle in the rocks. Nothing I'm thirsty enough to drink.''

Madison's thirst dulled. ''You dripped water you wouldn't drink *on my face?*'' Disgusted by the thought, she hastily scrubbed her fingers over the damp spots on her skin.

Linc caught her hand to stop her. ''Now you've made mud.'' One corner of his mouth kicked up in amusement.

Maddie glanced at her filthy fingers, horrified. Forgetting her dizziness, she searched the ground around them, spied the small suitcase, then shifted away from Linc to crawl the few inches on her hands and knees to get to it. She snapped it open and grabbed a hand mirror to check her face.

Grimy, finger-wide streaks punctuated by patches of sunburned skin ran across her forehead and down one cheek. Linc pushed the wet washcloth into her peripheral vision. Now more appalled by the ugly mud streaks than she was by the thought of dirty water, she snatched the cloth and used the mirror to guide a few well-aimed swipes at her skin.

But even when she'd finished, her face was anything but clean. Her mascara had run and flaked onto her cheekbones, her eyeshadow was smudged. There was no trace of foundation makeup or carefully applied blusher. Her lipstick had probably been the first thing to go.

She hastily tried to wipe away the remains of mascara beneath her eyes when she caught a glimpse of her hair. Leaf-dotted, tangled, and hanging in thin blond ropes, it was an utter mess.

She gave a groan of dismay, but before she could

do anything about it, the mirror and washcloth were plucked neatly from her fingers.

"Don't bother to make yourself pretty for me," Linc said rudely as he stowed the mirror and washcloth in the case and closed it. He took it with him when he stood. "We've only got another hour of light to find a stream and a place to sleep."

He reached down for her arm and hauled her to her feet. "And I damn sure hope you can walk on your own."

The man was a complete Neanderthal. Maddie hated that she had to cling to him for a moment while she struggled to steady herself. Her leg muscles were screaming with pain from the unaccustomed exertion, but they held her up. Her feet burned. By now, they were probably raw with broken blisters.

Linc let go of her then and picked up his duffel to add to her small case. Then he walked away from her without a backward glance. Worn out and annoyed, she realized with some surprise that her purse strap and the cord of her net bag were still securely crossed over her chest. She started after him, secretly relieved when he moderated his pace enough for her to keep up.

They'd almost lost the light before they heard the soft rushing sound of moving water. Linc came to an abrupt halt and froze to listen, and Maddie blundered into the arm he held out to stop her. She was so tired she was weaving on her feet.

"Come on."

Linc suddenly veered off to the left of the deer track they were on and instantly disappeared into the timber. Madison had to force herself to turn off the path to follow him. She fought her way through the undergrowth, battling to keep her hair and the net bag from catching on every bush and tree branch she passed.

At last she stepped around a tree and staggered to a halt to catch her breath. A swift-moving stream about six feet wide divided the narrow clearing. The bank was rocky in spots, but wide enough at one point that Linc was stretched out full-length on a flat boulder that jutted a few inches above the edge of the stream.

He'd left his Stetson with his duffel bag and her small case. Belly down on the rock, he was splashing cool, clear water on his face, heedless of how far behind him he flung the water.

Though she was dying of thirst, Madison took time to slip off her purse strap and the cord of the net bag to deposit them next to Linc's things before she joined him on the rock. The moment he realized she'd caught up with him, he stopped splashing. She knelt a couple feet away and leaned forward stiffly to brace one hand on the rock so she could reach the water with her other hand. She didn't care that she could feel Linc's eyes watching her every move.

Though the light was fading fast, she could see well enough to tell that her hand was too filthy to drink from. Desperate for a cool drink—but not *that* desperate—she edged closer to the water to wash her hands vigorously in the stream. She was so thirsty that she forgot the cake of soap in her suitcase and cupped her hand to bring a few swallows of water to her mouth.

At the last moment, sudden worry about the quality

of the water made her hesitate. The water leaked from her fingers.

"It's not purified water, sweetheart, but it's all right."

Madison flashed a weary glare in his direction for the pet name, then ignored him to try for another cupped hand of water. It took several before her thirst was partially quenched. By then, Linc had left the stream bank.

"Look around for more dry sticks," he called out when she sat back on her heels. She glanced over her shoulder at him, surprised to see that he'd already gathered a small pile of sticks and leaves. "Get movin' while you can still see your hand in front of your face."

Madison glanced at the dark timber that crowded densely alongside the stream bank. It was already hard to see. A good fire would give light, so she made herself get to her feet. She was so stiff she could barely walk. She found several sticks farther down the bank from Linc and was just leaning over to pick them up when a new thought sprang up to terrify her.

What if all of those sticks weren't wood? What if one of them was a snake? Though they hadn't seen a snake all day, they'd probably made enough noise tramping through the woods to scare them off. Madison straightened and kicked awkwardly at the loose sticks. Once she was certain that every stick *was* a stick, she leaned down stiffly to pick them up.

It was soon so dark she couldn't see at all, so she shuffled back painfully to the small fire with her collection of wood. She dropped it into a pile just as

Linc stepped into the small haze of light on the other side of the fire.

He carried a huge armload of dry wood. He'd selected several stout pieces that were easily as big around as his muscular arms, and when he dropped them on top of the puny pile she'd gathered, most of her contribution was smashed.

The casual destruction struck her as an insult, though she knew somewhere deep down that it wasn't intentional. Somehow it was the capstone to every fruitless struggle, every torment and frustration of the long day. Suddenly it all caught up to her with a vengeance; crushing hopelessness underscored everything.

She'd never get to Aspen in time. She'd resisted the thought for hours, but she couldn't escape it now. Her mother would never call her again; Roz would never give her another chance.

*Nothing in her life would ever change.* The bleak thought pounded at her. She had more money than she could ever spend, but no one to love who could possibly love her. Her history with her mother and her missing father proved that bitter truth and emphasized the existence of some fatal flaw that she would never overcome.

This missed opportunity with her mother dotted every *i* and crossed every *t* on the secret misery she lived with day in and day out, the misery of being unlovable. The injustice of it cut a jagged path across her heart and a black bile of bitterness oozed out. Bad temper roared up like a conflagration.

"Well, thanks a whole lot, *caveman*," she burst out. "Why did I waste my time finding those sticks?"

Untroubled by her outburst, Linc crouched down on the other side of the fire and placed two of the larger pieces of wood onto the flames. His handsome mouth curved indulgently at her pique, and it infuriated her.

"All right, sweetheart," he drawled. "You've been savin' it all day. Let's get this little tantrum out of the way—but make it a good one so you won't have anything left to gripe about later."

His mouth was still slanted in an indulgent line and his dark eyes glittered over at her with amusement. He was deliberately provocative and he knew it.

*Of all the condescending, arrogant...* Maddie's temper shot sky-high.

"Oh, *yes,*" she agreed, starting off in a sarcastically sweet voice that gradually increased in volume. "Let's get this little tantrum out of the way...*Ace.*" She gave him a poisonous smile. "The tantrum *you're* entirely responsible for, *Mr. Macho* run - her - through - the - woods - so - fast - that - the - shoes - *you* - made - her - wear - rub - holes - in - her - feet."

The amused slant of his mouth went a bit flatter. The small indication that she'd pricked his ego urged her on.

"Let's start with that toy airplane, *Sky King*. What was wrong with it anyway?" she asked in the scathing tone she'd perfected these last years. "Did the rubber band break?

"As for your skills as a pilot, you could have just as easily turned the damned thing toward the plains where we had *some* chance of being seen and attracting a rescue.

"And now that I think about it, what happened to

the radio?'' Her voice had grown more demanding, more angry with every word. ''Does anyone know we're stuck up here? Did you bother to file a flight plan, or were you too macho?

''Which brings me to the next logical question: Why don't you have a cell phone like every other millionaire in Texas? Is it too complicated for a Neanderthal like you to operate?''

Her rising voice suddenly dropped to a scornful feminine growl. ''And you really *are* a Neanderthal, you know. *Linc*oln Coryell—*Linc* Coryell—*Linc*.'' She lifted her light brows and cocked her head mockingly as she bounded miles past the limit. ''Is that L-i-n-c? Or is it L-i-n-k, as in *the missing link?*

''And while we're on the subject of your background,'' she railed on, now practically shouting at him, ''do you still have some primitive connection to nature and a sense of direction, or are we destined to wander in this wilderness until we're both wearing animal skins and living in a cave?''

Madison's tirade abruptly ran down as a huge wave of dizziness swept over her. She was shaking, swaying on unsteady legs, feeling somehow distanced from herself. Was she going to faint?

The night sounds of the forest began to creep back into her awareness then, as if they'd stopped during her tirade, and had only now found the courage to start up again. The sound of crickets and cicadas, the pop and crackle of the fire—all combined to form a peculiar new tension that seemed to both center on Lincoln Coryell and radiate from him.

He hadn't taken his dark eyes off her, though that indulgent, condescending smile that had so infuriated her had long since flattened to a grim line. The air between them was suddenly charged with what Madison could only believe was active dislike. But so what? She hated him more than he could ever hate her.

Without a word, Linc rose from the other side of the fire and slowly straightened to his full six-foot-four-plus height. He reached up with that same measured slowness and took off his Stetson, letting it drop carelessly to the ground near the heels of his big boots. His dark eyes hadn't moved a fraction off hers.

His Texas drawl was low and gravelly with purpose. "Sounds like someone needs to make an effort with you, Miz Maddie." He started slowly around the fire.

Madison couldn't move as he advanced. The wordless menace of his approach mesmerized her. She was suddenly so terrified of him—his face was like carved granite—that the terror of the crash and its aftermath now seemed like nothing more than mild anxiety.

"As someone from my background might say, 'It's high time someone brought that little filly in from the range and put her under a saddle.'" His eyes were burning as darkly as the fire. "Let's see if you can be broke to ride."

Those last inches vanished the moment he reached for her, swung her into his arms and stalked away from the fire. Madison braced her hands against his chest in self-protection.

"How *dare* you put your hands on me! Put me down, you giant ape!" She was pushing away with all her might when he abruptly dropped her.

The sharp fall into the freezing water of the stream

startled a shriek out of her. The surface of the water broke her fall, then swallowed her up to her shoulders. The cold made her gasp, and she thrashed wildly to get her feet under her so she could stand up.

But the stream bottom was slick, and the darkness was disorienting. She floundered, sputtering and gasping out insults, until she managed to dunk herself completely beneath the wet surface. When she could finally turn over and get on her knees, she had to fight to get to her feet in the shallow water.

Once she could stand up, Linc towered over her, looming close as if he were seriously thinking about shoving her down and holding her head under the surface. Choking on the water she'd swallowed, and more furious than ever, Madison doubled up her fist and took an ill-advised swing at him.

Her punch never landed. Linc merely raised his hand and gave her shoulder a little push. It wasn't much of a push, but it was enough to send her off balance. She shrieked again as she lost her footing and went down for another icy dunk.

This time, Linc only let her flounder for a few moments before he grabbed her upper arms and hauled her to her feet.

She came up choking. "You bully!"

Linc caught her wrists before she could take another swing at him. Maddie tried to kick him, but her legs were trembling with fatigue and the water dragged too much on her clothes and body for her to do more than nudge the ankle of his boot with the toe of her shoe.

The leg she was balanced on was too weak against the current of the stream, and her foot slipped. If Linc hadn't had a firm hold on her wrists, she would have dunked herself again. As it was, she dipped into water to her waist before she could get both feet under her again.

"Give it up, you little hellion," he said with gruff humor as he gave her a small shake. "Even a bronc knows when to stop fighting."

"I'm no horse!" she burst out, but her strength was nearly gone. She could barely stand. Her exhausted gaze came up to meet his, but her defiance still burned bright. "And you're no Horse Whisperer!"

He chuckled then. A low, masculine sound that was entirely too warm and appealing.

"So you understand that I won't let myself get stomped to death at the end of this story. That's the first real sign of hope I've seen in you, Princess." He pulled her closer, and her breath caught. "Come on, let's get you rubbed down and put up for the night."

# CHAPTER FOUR

*LET'S GET YOU RUBBED DOWN...*

The images that stormed through her mind were shockingly sexual and Madison was instantly on guard. She was so weak now that she would be completely at his mercy. He had a firm grip and she couldn't possibly free herself.

What kind of man was Lincoln Coryell, really? The very idea that any man could overpower her and force himself on her was an alien one. But he'd just shown her how physically ineffectual she was against him. What if he decided to make a pass? They were completely alone out here. Proximity was enough for some men.

She'd never considered herself vulnerable to sexual danger. She was vigilant about her personal safety and knew without a doubt that the confident image she projected discouraged most miscreants from marking her as a victim. Her independent attitude and abrasive personality intimidated most men and successfully kept them at a safe distance.

She'd just given Linc a demonstration of shrewish strong will that should have sent him running for the trees. Instead, he seemed completely unfazed. He started for the bank with her in tow.

Linc's touch was having a bizarre effect on her. How could she be frightened of him, yet almost glow with the electric thrill of his touch? Was she so hungry for affection in her emotionally isolated life that she was easy prey for any reasonably attractive man? Even one who'd made the crude comparison between breaking a horse to ride and getting the upper hand with her? She was losing her mind!

Wary of Linc and the bewildering excitement he stirred in her, Madison began to pull back on his tight hold. He paused at her resistance and casually brought her hands together. Just that quickly, he wrapped the fingers of one big hand around both her wrists at once, then started forward again, dragging her out of the water like a prisoner.

Her apprehension multiplied at this new demonstration of superior strength. She was absolutely appalled that the macho display sent a delicious quiver of sensual peril through her.

Never mind asking what kind of man he was— what kind of woman was she?

Once she was on dry ground, she tried to brace her feet and twist out of his grip. It was impossible until he suddenly released her. Madison stumbled backward and almost suffered the fresh indignity of falling on her rear.

"Get those clothes off."

The brusque order horrified her. She glanced around the circle of light. Everything outside its golden perimeter was black with shadows and unseen danger. Though she understood the necessity of getting dry—the mountain air was rapidly cooling— there was absolutely no privacy.

The remark he'd made about rubbing her down made another pass through her mind and sent another shock of excitement through her.

Madison looked on apprehensively while he pried off his boots. His jeans were wet. Her eyes went wide when he reached for his belt. Unselfconscious, he unbuckled it and stripped it out of the loops with a snap. When he reached for the metal button of his jeans, her gaze flinched away.

*He was about to take off his pants!* The soft burr of the zipper going down made her turn her back on him completely and hobble to the very edge of the light.

*Oh, God, what next?* Maddie stared desperately into the shadowy trees that marked the boundary between gloomy light and absolute blackness. The cool night air seeped through her sodden clothes and leached the heat from her body. She was freezing.

"You can either wear your robe—" Linc's voice startled her, "—which I don't advise considering our sleeping arrangements—or you can change into your clean clothes."

Madison dared a quick glance over her shoulder. Linc was wearing a pair of dry jeans. He hadn't tucked in the tail of his shirt, but he was decently clothed.

Some of her worry eased until he added, "I refuse to cuddle up to a wet lump, so get a move on."

The terse words alarmed her. "You can cuddle up to the nearest porcupine for all I care," she retorted, compelled to thwart any notions he might have about associating the word "cuddle" with her. Now if she could just do the same, she'd feel as if she was gaining some ground on sanity.

He flashed her a look. "Lady, every word out of your mouth comes out a dare. One of these days, some man with more sand than sense is going to take you up on it.''

The sensual threat was there. Why was everything suddenly so sexual? Desperate to bring back the prickly distance of mutual dislike, Maddie lifted her chin a fraction to assert herself.

''Spare me your folksy analogies, cowboy. Only a man who's so weak he feels compelled to constantly prove and defend his manhood sees a dare in every conversation.''

One corner of his mouth quirked. ''If talk like that is your way of comin' on to me, you need to know that I've got a rare affection for a challenge. And when one comes along that's tied close to the possibility of sex, it's damned near irresistible.''

The declaration alarmed her. The primitive feminine reaction it set off sent a sweet sting of dread and excitement through her that made her want to scream with frustration.

''There is no sexual challenge here.'' She enunciated every word in another desperate attempt to get his mind off the subject of sex. But her brain was suddenly obsessed with it. The sight of his big virile body brought back every memory of her unintentional contact with him.

His dark eyes took on an intensity that made her breath catch. Slowly, deliberately, his gaze went over her, from the crown of her head to the toes of her Nikes. When it lingered meaningfully in significant places, her blood pounded wildly in her ears.

''No sexual challenge, huh?'' His gaze slowly retraced its path to her heated face. ''Sassy, blond and beautiful, with all the right curves in all the right places.''

His eyes fixed on her chest as he bluntly chronicled what he saw.

''Wet clothes. *Clinging* wet clothes. Lush... attributes. Chilly mountain air that brings out—''

Appalled, Maddie glanced down at her wet red blouse and gasped. Despite the water-darkened red color, she might as well have been naked from the waist up. She grabbed the front of her blouse and pulled the soggy fabric away from her skin.

''So now you see another important reason to change into dry clothes,'' he remarked. ''I'll turn my back 'til you're done.''

Maddie's head jerked up and she searched his face closely. She trusted him even less than she had before. Her body was tingling from his shocking physical inventory. What was going on in his?

Her teeth began to chatter convulsively, and she was suddenly aware that she was freezing to death. She had absolutely no choice but to trust him not to look—not to pounce—while she changed her clothes. She was so cold she could barely speak.

''H-how do I kn-know you w-won't look-k?''

His strong mouth tightened and his dark gaze went a little hard. ''Because I give you my word.''

Something in her relaxed at that. Lincoln Coryell had a reputation for keeping his word. But did his strong public integrity extend to the wilderness isolation of the Rocky Mountains?

Linc looked away from her anxious face and walked over to their pile of belongings. He picked up the net bag and threw it across the fire to her. Madison caught it reflexively and clutched it to the front of her.

His dark gaze lingered on her face a few moments more before he turned his back and walked to the edge of the firelight.

The change into dry clothes warmed her for only a little while. Hovering close to the fire made her sunburned face feel like it was blistering, and the heat made her head swim with sleepiness.

Nothing was said about food. At least Linc had given her a flashlight from his duffel bag so she could walk away from camp for a long-awaited call of nature. She'd been terrified of going so far in the darkness, even with a flashlight, but she'd found complete privacy and she'd survived the trip.

Now she was doing her best to stay awake and ignore Linc while the front of her got too hot and her back chilled. She looked on when he unrolled the piece of plastic and spread it out on the other side of the fire from where she sat. The plastic sheet was wider than a double bed. He unfolded the lone blanket next and laid it on top of the plastic.

He'd draped his damp jeans over a nearby tree branch, but he'd used the rope to fashion a clothesline for her wet things. They were stretched out on the tree side of the fire so they'd be dry by morning.

His consideration—and the subtle demonstration of concern for her clothing over his—shamed her a little. Maybe she'd misjudged him. Perhaps she'd gone overboard with her scathing remarks about him being a Neanderthal. She shouldn't have criticized him about the plane crash either. He'd at least gotten them down without getting them killed.

But she kept her part of the tense, heavy silence of the campsite. The "sex talk" of more than an hour ago had ended. Maddie hoped nothing remotely sexual remained in his mind, though she was still having trouble with hers.

Sleepiness and exhaustion seemed to heighten the warm sensuality that lingered in the wake of it all. The soft golden glow of the fire made a definite contribution to the feeling.

Linc was totally unsuitable for her. Every man she'd met since Beau had been unsuitable. No one had ever measured up to the ideal Beau had set.

But suddenly it was Linc who was setting the standard for attraction. The disloyal thoughts to Beau's memory upset her. Linc upset her. She had to force herself not to examine too closely what it was about him that disrupted her. But without anything but him to focus her mind on, it was a struggle.

The makeshift bed was finished. Linc had dragged the duffel bag over, probably to use as a crude pillow. She watched him, wondering how he'd solved the problem of their sleeping arrangements. She'd made her thoughts on the subject clear, so she wasn't worried about where he was going to sleep.

Until he straightened and his dark gaze found hers across the fire.

"Time to turn in."

The terse words gave her a small jolt. Now his remark about not wanting to cuddle up to a wet lump made a lightning pass through her brain cells. Something told her he had no intention of sleeping anywhere but on that blanket, in spite of what she'd said earlier.

Her, "We can't sleep together," was instant.

"We've got one blanket and an air temperature that'll probably fall at least another ten degrees. Unless you remembered to reserve a room at the local motel, you don't have a choice."

"Sleeping together isn't an option."

"It's the only option," he countered. "D'you want to get into a wrestling match, or would you rather just lie down and get some sleep?"

The memory of being completely at his mercy in the stream was still strong. The grim look he was giving her was a solemn promise that he was willing to manhandle her again to ensure her cooperation.

Maddie suddenly felt helpless and trapped. It didn't matter that she was wildly attracted to Linc. The odd sense that this was somehow connected to the unhappiness of her life was strong and suddenly profound.

She'd been a helpless child once, with no real choices. She'd been trapped in a painful, dismal existence with caretakers who should have loved her, but couldn't because she was somehow not worthy.

Linc couldn't possibly care; she knew he hated her. He, too, saw her as a burden, a drag on his effort to get out of the mountains. And now he was trapping her—forcing her to lie next to him wrapped in a blanket for the night.

The implied intimacy of it was something she secretly craved, yet was terrified to allow. Because she was so attracted to him, she couldn't handle his closeness, couldn't cope with the sexual implications of such sleeping arrangements. She also couldn't handle the notion of craving something from him, perhaps even getting it, only to have him roll out of the blanket in the morning still not liking her and still weighted down by the duty and burden of her existence.

She was still staring at him, making no move to get to her feet and comply, when he started toward her. In her belated rush to stand and get away from him, she gasped at the sharp pain of moving. Her body had gone so stiff that she could barely get up. Her legs were twin extensions of agony, and her feet were so sore that she could only limp a couple of short steps before he reached her.

"Stay away from me!"

The hasty words were her only chance of warding him off. Impatience made a quick pass over his face, but he stopped.

"How bad are those feet?" The low sound of his voice carried a wisp of concern that eased her panic. She'd already decided he might not be a complete Neanderthal, but this infinitesimal hint of worry warmed something vulnerable in her.

On the other hand, if her feet were too sore, she presented a new problem for him. She would be even more of a burden if she couldn't walk. Or worse, if he had to carry her. The little bit of warmth went cold.

"Not bad at all." She took a couple more agonizing steps. She'd put on clean socks but left her shoes to dry. Her feet hurt too much to try the hiking boots just yet and she hated that walking around the campsite would get her socks dirty.

Linc's stern mouth slanted a little, but the telltale quirk of one side fairly shouted his cynicism.

"You're turning out to be quite a liar, Miz Maddie."

Madison was about to make an acid retort when he leaned down and plucked her off the ground. He swung her up into his arms so fast that she clutched his broad shoulders to steady herself. She was too stiff to fight him as he carried her to the other side of the fire and sat her on top of the blanket. He released her to slide a hand down the leg of her jeans to seize her foot before she could make a move to get up.

Maddie couldn't stifle a groan when he crouched down and lifted her sore leg to examine her foot. The feel of his long, hard fingers pushing up the inside of her jeans leg to catch the top of her sock sent a shiver of tingles over her skin that impacted deep in every feminine spot on her body. His grip on her ankle was too strong for her to jerk away.

Linc peeled the sock down and she sucked in a breath. The small sound made him stop.

"Damn it, Maddie—"

He'd discovered that the thick sock had stuck to the raw skin of a broken blister. He gently pulled it loose, then finished taking the sock off slowly as he watched for other raw spots. Once her foot was bare and he'd examined it, he swore softly. He lowered her ankle and set her foot down on the blanket before he let go.

"You've got a drugstore in that case, and you haven't used a damned bit of it on this." His dark eyes were blazing. "How the hell do you think you're going to walk tomorrow without doing something about this tonight?"

He didn't wait for an answer, but stood up to fetch

her small case. He was back with it and had it open before she could think of escape.

Linc sorted through her things, but she was too weary now to worry about it. He set out a small tube of antibiotic cream and a box of assorted bandages. In moments, he'd lifted her foot. The angle made her leg hurt and she leaned back to brace herself on her elbows to relieve the ache.

His hands were hard and callused and warm. His fingers were stunningly gentle as he smoothed the cream on her heel, over her instep and gave special attention to her two smallest toes, which had been particularly abused.

Maddie caught her breath when he eased her foot down to rest her ankle on his thigh. He tore open a packaged gauze square and used her tiny nail scissors to cut it into fourths.

The sight of his big fingers wielding the miniature scissors made her realize how capable he was, even with small things. When he finished with the scissors, he lightly pressed the gauze patches to the thick layer of cream he'd applied.

He picked up her sock then, and efficiently rolled it into a donut shape before he carefully eased it onto her toes. He unrolled it until her foot and ankle were covered and the gauze patches safely anchored.

By the time he started on her other foot, she'd sunk back to lie flat on the blanket to watch him. Her eyelids were almost too heavy to keep open.

Linc's touch was easily the most seductive thing she'd ever experienced. She'd never imagined that the languorous sensuality that washed over her in wave after delicious wave was even possible. There was no

evidence of his dislike for her on his face now. Only
an intensity that suggested concern and compassion.

Her hungry heart gobbled it up, torn between stuff-
ing itself with everything it could get, and savoring
every sweet morsel. Maddie's eyes stung. She'd been
so lonely, so painfully alone. She hadn't been touched
for years, and couldn't remember ever being touched
like this. Not even by Beau. Beau, who'd seemed so
interested in touching her in far more personal and
sexual places.

My God, was this what it was like to be cared for,
to have some semblance of sexless physical affection
from another human being?

Linc was lavishing his attention and his touch on
her feet—her *feet!* Hardly the sexual target of a lover,
and yet suddenly the most erotically charged spot on
her body.

Her eyes stung harder. She was so pitiful that she
was getting emotional and turned on over a man
touching her feet! Her pride wasn't strong enough to
give her heart the bracing slap it needed. So she lay
there, her eyes closed, soaking up every sensation,
every bit of emotional sustenance she could.

When Linc at last set her foot on the blanket, it
was all she could do not to cry out at the loss of his
touch. The reminder that he'd soon be lying next to
her kept her silent and motionless with suspense. She
hated the thought that she was suddenly eager for
more from him, but she couldn't seem to stop herself.

Maddie listened while Linc put things away in her
case and closed it. He must have set it out of the way
someplace close, because she felt the difference in the

air as he leaned toward her and shifted to lie down alongside her.

The heat of his big body was welcome. And then she felt him turn toward her. The blanket settled over her from shoulders to feet. His warm breath gusted softly on her face when he spoke.

"You look like a trembling virgin who thinks the big bad outlaw is about to ravage her."

The gruff words were edged with humor. Maddie's eyes popped open. Linc was leaning over her, his handsome mouth less than two hand spans from hers.

The firelight played over the planes and angles of his face, sharpening some, softening others. His eyes were so dark that they glittered with the golden firelight reflected in their depths.

Maddie didn't dare respond to his remark. She'd hardly been lying there terrified. The sight of his strong, handsome features, the incredible heat from his body, the whisper-light feeling of his breath on her face—

After several minutes of him touching her feet, it was all she could do to keep from begging him to touch her anywhere he liked, however he liked, however long he wanted to.

Her gaze focused on his lips. The raw craving to feel their pressure, to taste them, made her ache. She hadn't been kissed in forever. Instinct told her that Linc's kisses would be skilled and experienced, and they'd be wielded with far more maturity and masculine authority than eighteen-year-old Beau Duvall's ever had.

Beau was suddenly a wisp of thought, a faceless memory. The sight of Linc—his overpowering male presence—banished clear thoughts of anyone or anything else. She didn't even care that they were lying on the hard ground surrounded by miles of trees and mountains and dangerous animals.

Linc's hand eased against her side, his hard fingers curving around her ribs. Maddie's breath caught as his hand moved slowly up, then stopped just beneath her breast. His eyes were so intense, so turbulent with desire, that she knew he was about to kiss her. Every atom of her body was straining toward him, so starved for him that it was all she could do to lie quietly and wait.

What he said to her then was a rude dash of cold reality.

"I got the virgin part right, but I'm not so sure you're dreading anything," he said roughly. "I guess you aren't quite the challenge I thought."

With that, he moved his hand, then shifted and lay down, taking a moment to drag the duffel bag into place under his head.

Madison lay in shock, so profoundly disappointed that her chest thudded with it. Linc hadn't kissed her, hadn't even tried. She'd been so sure he'd been about to, but he not only hadn't followed through, he'd dealt her a colossal insult.

The careless rejection stole her breath and she had to concentrate fiercely to take air into her lungs and force it out at anything close to a normal rhythm.

Her heart withered then. The hopelessness she normally was able to cope with settled over her like a smothering weight.

Why had she been so afraid of the plane going

down? Why had she been so terrified at the thought of sudden death in the crash?

Her eyelids drooped closed, then squeezed tight for a few excruciating moments. Her mother was lost to her forever, along with everyone else important to her. Even if she somehow made up with Caitlin, Cait was married now and had a full, happy life. Maddie's presence in her cousin's future would likely never be a bright spot for Caitlin after years of estrangement.

The pain of being certain that no one would ever really want her, that it wasn't possible for anyone to love her or to allow her to pour out her love on them, was almost more than she could bear.

As she made herself turn on her side and face away from Linc, she put as many inches as she could between her aching body and the wonderful heat and feel of his.

She'd never be afraid of death again. The only thing it could change in her life was the elevation.

Linc's big body was humming like a tuning fork. What in hell had he been thinking? Madison St. John, in spite of her prickly ways, was turning out to be more temptation than he was used to.

She was attracted to him, but she'd fought it all day. He'd come to expect it. But the thought of being wrapped all night in a blanket with her choice little body had made him eager to get one last rise out of her, one more sharp little set-down. Somehow he'd needed a fresh reminder of how unsuited they were to each other, how difficult she was to get along with.

He'd felt her melt when he'd doctored her feet, but she'd been exhausted, so he'd discounted the sleepy way she'd watched him, he'd ignored the sense that something had changed in her. But then he'd looked down into her huge blue eyes and seen the welcome and anticipation of a woman who couldn't wait for his kiss.

His body had responded swiftly and painfully. He'd had to put a stop to it right away, and he hadn't been too particular about how he'd got the job done.

He realized now that he'd hurt her feelings. She'd made no acid retort, she'd not made a single sound. She'd just lain there quietly, closed her eyes, then a few seconds later, she'd rolled away from him. She was lying so far from him now that the edge of the blanket barely covered her.

He'd wait until he was sure she was asleep before he pulled her closer and made certain she had enough of the blanket to keep her warm.

He'd make doubly sure that there'd be no more close calls. He was no longer curious about whether Madison St. John was a frigid little witch or not.

He'd stumbled onto the answer. And because he'd sensed something else—that Maddie's prickly exterior was the cover for a well of vulnerability—she wasn't a woman to toy with unless he had serious feelings for her.

# CHAPTER FIVE

MORNING CAME TOO QUICKLY. Maddie rolled away from the light and shielded her eyes with the blanket. She fell back to sleep and must have lain there for some time before she was prodded awake. The sun was much brighter this time.

"Come on, Sleeping Beauty, breakfast is almost ready." Linc's drawl came from somewhere high above her. "Take your walk in the woods and get back before it gets cold."

*Food.* Her empty stomach clenched. She struggled to turn over and sit up before she realized what the food smell was.

*Fish.* Identifying it made the agony of forcing her abused body to move so much worse. She *hated* fish.

Her hesitation got Linc's attention. "Your boots are beside you." She glanced over at him. He was crouched on the other side of the fire from her now.

Her gaze caught on the two forked sticks that poked up on either side of the fire with another stick resting across their notches. Five headless, tailless fish had been impaled on the horizontal stick and hung over the fire to cook. She grimaced at the sight and looked away to reach for a boot.

When she took hold of it to drag to her lap, she noticed that Linc had put the leather laces back in. The thoughtful gesture rubbed her wrong. She was rarely a cheerful riser these days, but for some reason, the fact that he'd done something considerate for her rankled.

Maybe because she knew he didn't like her, *couldn't* like her. So why torture her with kind acts that she might mistake for something they were never meant to be?

She managed to bend one stiff knee to get her foot close enough to slip on the boot. Pride made her keep her sullen thoughts to herself. She'd slept the night through, but she was still so tired that she felt slow and otherworldly. And she hurt. Her stomach hurt with hunger. Moving hurt. Putting on the boot hurt. And the sun was so bright that her eyeballs hurt.

Linc looked on as Maddie gathered up the leather laces to tighten them. He knew the moment she realized the laces were wet. Her frown darkened.

"How did these get wet?" she groused, her voice still raspy from sleep.

"The white laces from your other shoes scared the fish off," he drawled.

Maddie froze and a comic look of disgust crossed her face. She dropped the laces to inspect her fingers. "You used my boot laces to catch fish?"

Her voice was still raspy, but disbelief gave it an ominous undertone. No doubt about it, she was a sissy. A cranky sissy. And spoiled rotten.

But beautiful. Rumpled, witchy, her hair tangled like a pile of straw, but still sexy and appealing. A fresh taste of her poison personality might be just what he needed to smother the lingering sensual thrill of lying next to her all night. She was so easily riled.

"Probably need them to catch supper," he said casually.

Maddie's head jerked up and she looked over at him, her expression a mix of anger and shock. "You didn't use worms to catch the fish, did you?"

The revulsion on her face amused him and he felt the start of a smile. "You were still sleeping, so we couldn't use your charming personality."

Maddie's cheeks flushed. "You put my laces near worms?"

*The woman was rabidly neurotic.*

"Technically, the worm was hooked on one of your safety pins. Probably never touched the laces."

Maddie gave him a surly look. "You handled my laces with wormy fingers."

"And if we see some rabbits, we'll use them to build a snare."

Her expression switched to alarm. "You'd use my laces to kill a rabbit."

Maddie didn't state it as a question, but as an accusation. She could see for herself—knew by last night's experience—that Lincoln Coryell could do, would do, anything he pleased with anyone—or any-*thing*—he wanted. But Maddie couldn't stand for him to kill a rabbit. And how would he do it? A bullet would mean a swift death, and the rabbit might not suffer the fear of being caught or even know it was being hunted if it was shot.

But a rabbit caught in a snare would suffer terrible fear. It would know it was about to die. How would Linc kill it then? Strangulation? Would he hit it with a rock? It was too awful to consider.

"You don't need to kill a harmless little rabbit. I don't eat meat."

Her declaration got a quick answer.

"Maybe if you ate meat once in a while, you wouldn't take so many bites out of other people."

The blunt statement made her breath catch.

"And before you start on another *how dare you* snit, get your boots on and take your hike." He glanced pointedly at her hair. "You might take a minute after breakfast to brush through those tangles and check yourself for ticks."

Maddie's ire abruptly vanished. She forgot the imaginary rabbit and its cruel fate. Her lips parted briefly in fresh surprise. "Ticks?"

"Regular wood ticks might not hurt you, but we should get 'em off anyway. It's those little ticks..." His voice fell away with disturbing significance.

Maddie swallowed hard at the matter-of-fact words. "*Little* ticks?"

"Deer ticks cause Lyme Disease, the others cause Rocky Mountain Spotted Fever. Might be they're the same kind of tick. I'm no expert, but some are real small. You have to look closer for those."

He paused to reach for the stick that held the fish and adjusted it. "If we check ourselves morning and night, there shouldn't be a problem. Just don't pull 'em out. We'll try some of your polish remover to get 'em to let go."

Terror descended over Maddie. Suddenly she could feel ticks crawling everywhere under her clothes and in her hair. She'd never given ticks a thought. Bears and mountain lions and wolves maybe, but not ticks.

Linc had just given her a whole new nightmare to cope with.

My God—you could die from Lyme Disease and Rocky Mountain Spotted Fever!

Her horror must have shown on her face because Linc's mouth quirked sardonically. "No need to fret. Even if you got bit by a bad tick, we'll likely be able to get to a doctor in plenty of time to keep you from getting sick."

The remark sank in slowly past her fear. And pricked her temper. "They why even mention them?"

"You gotta use your head out here."

Aggravated, but less terrorized, she looked away and tried to focus on getting her boots on and the wet laces tied. Finally, she struggled to her feet. With no help from her tormentor, who seemed annoyingly interested in her every move. She did her best to ignore him and hoped he felt snubbed.

The effort of standing up made her fully aware that she was a mass of misery from head to foot. The dandy little headache that started made her discomfort complete. Several cautious steps around the campsite loosened her abused leg muscles enough for her to find her way to the same narrow trail into the timber that she'd used the night before.

She was well into the trees when Linc called after her. "Be on the lookout for poison ivy and poison sumac."

Madison was certain then that she'd died in the plane crash after all, because her worst fears had been realized: *she'd landed in hell.*

Maddie hurt so much she could barely hobble along. It was late afternoon and her stomach felt like a hundred-gallon barrel filled with nothing but empty space. It was as if the few bites of fish she'd forced on herself that morning had never existed.

She'd been foolish to spurn the generous portion of cooked meat Linc had allotted her. She'd nibbled a few bites, then given the rest to him. But, what she'd give now for one mouthful of the hideous little things!

The only good thing was that her skin didn't crawl with imaginary ticks anymore. She didn't have the phantom poison ivy itches either. Instead, she'd become a head-to-toe bundle of numbing pain. Even the sunblock that she'd applied fanatically to face, hands and arms had failed. She'd probably suffered untold damage to her fair complexion.

And Linc walked ahead of her as if he was still as fresh and strong as when they'd started out.

They'd walked forever—easily *hundreds* of miles. Today the land was flatter than it had been the day before on their way down the mountain. They'd crossed two valleys that had looked small next to the mountains, but had turned out to seem miles long.

She'd somehow lost her perspective of distance. Everything—the mountains, the trees, some stray boulder or rock outcropping here or there—seemed to loom close until she was actually walking toward it. Then everything appeared to back up, making it impossible to get anywhere fast.

Maybe out here where no one else could see, nature just sort of shifted the mountains and trees away from you the harder you tried to reach them. A Rocky Mountain mirage. More insidious than the water mirages on a long strip of highway, but just as illusive and aggravating.

At least they were in the trees again, out of the full sun. They were moving parallel to a wide creek. Maybe the same one they'd found last night, maybe another. She had no sense of direction now.

She needed a cool drink, a table-load of food, a bath, and about a week's worth of sleep and medical attention. The Valium prescription she'd bullied out of her doctor to smooth out her nerves in case things went wrong with her mother was still in Linc's shirt pocket. Though she'd rarely taken Valium, this whole awful adventure seemed tailor-made for tranquilizers. On the other hand, she hadn't had a breakdown yet, so perhaps she was sturdier than she'd thought.

But that could be because the terror and hardship of the wilderness seemed so much less upsetting than the potential for emotional calamity she'd been willing to risk with her mother. The reminder that her no-show would embarrass Roz in front of her new family made her insides churn.

Roz might never find out that she hadn't done it on purpose; she'd be so angry she'd never call again. No one except Maddie's staff knew she'd decided to go to Colorado, and though they knew, they wouldn't be able to tell Roz if she didn't call the mansion to check. Her mother's calls were too infrequent. Her call on Friday morning was probably Maddie's allotment for the year. Maybe the last for a lifetime.

Maddie had dismissed her chauffeur before she'd got the flight with Linc, so no one at the mansion would suspect that she'd been in a plane crash even if they found out that Linc's plane had gone down.

The other pilot would have no reason to tell anyone that she was flying with Linc unless he learned that Linc's plane had crashed. But then, he might not know for sure that Linc had actually allowed her to fly with him. No one had been around when she'd got in Linc's plane.

Why hadn't she told her mother right away that she'd come to Colorado instead of indulging her pride and being vague? And why hadn't she called her mother to let her know she was on her way? Roz hadn't left a number, but she could have gotten it from Information. Why hadn't she thought of these things when they might have done her some good? Now her mother had no certain idea that she was coming, no set time to worry if she didn't show up.

If Roz had ever really worried about her. The depressing thought dragged her heart down. No one would miss her, no one would care if she was never found.

Even Linc hated having her around. He was thriving in the wilderness. Cooking over an open fire, sleeping on the hard ground, tramping through the woods, fishing with her shoelaces. It was all a big macho adventure to him.

She'd tried to get him to stop for a while so she could take off her boots and maybe wade in the stream, but he'd ignored her. Her feet felt as if they'd swelled to the size of basketballs and the sting of the raw blisters was agonizing. The last time she'd tried to get him to stop, he'd called her a whiner.

So she wasn't speaking to him anymore. She'd run through a wickedly creative repertoire of insults by noon. After that, she'd realized that he couldn't hear them from so far ahead anyway, so the effort wasn't worth the waste of energy and precious breath.

When Linc suddenly disappeared up ahead, she felt a quiver of unease. She'd kept him in sight the whole day, but only because he wasn't out to set a land speed record like he had the day before.

Where had he gone? Maddie's sluggish steps speeded up. He'd stepped off the path, but she wasn't sure where. She was just summoning the energy to call out when she felt something step in close behind her.

Something big and strong and overpowering grabbed her, swinging her off the path and dragging her into the trees so fast that she could only gasp. A hard male hand clamped over her mouth before she could scream.

The low growl of Linc's voice was both terrifying and welcome. "Run, damn it, or you're going to be supper."

Maddie couldn't think, she could only react. Though she was exhausted and so stiff she could barely walk, she suddenly came alive, stumbling between the trees at an awkward run to escape the nameless danger that lurked somewhere behind them. Linc slid his hand off her mouth and stopped pushing. He grabbed her arm and jerked her along with him up the steep incline away from the stream. His grip on her arm was tight and painful, but she didn't care as long as he took her with him. Her legs gave out just as they got to the top. Her lungs were on fire and working like a bellows. Her head was swimming and her knees were too rubbery to hold her up. Terror made her nauseous.

Whatever they were running from would get her now! Linc couldn't possibly carry her and save himself. And he would never sacrifice himself for her. The bear—it couldn't be anything less than a bear—would get her. Her! Madison St. John, grabbed and eaten by a bear! Why couldn't she have died in the plane crash! Oh God!

Linc let her collapse, though he guided her down and didn't let her land hard. Why didn't he just let her fall? He could use the time to get away. While the bear was busy gobbling her up, he could run miles.

A sob of pure terror jerked her body and tore at her chest and dry throat. She glanced back in horror expecting to see the bear, but there was nothing behind them. She floundered a moment, trying to use some bit of strength to get on her feet while there was still a small chance of getting away, but Linc held her down.

"It's all right now," he told her. "Look there." He gestured down the incline to the right through a break in the trees. They could see a bit of the stream from their high vantage point. After a moment, a huge brown bear lumbered into view. "No way of tellin' if he'd had supper or not, so it was best to just get the hell away before he caught wind of us."

Maddie had been lying on her side with her elbow braced under her to rise, but the fact that she'd been saved from the bear drained the terror and tension from her body. Because it was far away now and seemed not to realize they were nearby, she was so monumentally relieved that she turned to her stomach and lay flat, resting her cheek on her forearm as she tried to catch her breath.

"Iyeee *hate* this." Maddie's voice was a dry, feminine growl, but there was no sound of tears.

Linc had to hand it to her. She complained loudly and frequently when she was unhappy, but she wasn't a crybaby. She'd been through a hell of a lot for a pampered aristocrat, but other than that little sob of fear when she couldn't run anymore and thought she was going to die, she hadn't dissolved in a puddle of tears. He couldn't help but admire the steely substance that was mixed in with all that fire and vinegar.

"When you get your breath back, we'll go on through these trees up here until we're far enough past the bear to find a campsite."

Maddie was still puffing for breath, but she got out, "How will we know when we're far enough away?"

"We'll check the stream bank for paw prints. That should give us some sign we aren't camped at a bear's favorite watering spot."

Maddie was comforted by the common sense answer. Obviously, Linc was a thinking man. Though it hadn't entered her mind, it was logical to look for paw prints along a stream bed. Linc might not be well educated, but it was clear that he was quite intelligent.

But then, he'd made himself a millionaire several times over, so whatever he'd needed for success hadn't required a college degree, or even a high school diploma.

She'd sensed all along that he was smarter than she was and more capable, but she hadn't wanted to give him credit for it. Her world was much safer and less painful when she was the superior one, the absolute ruler.

Maybe it was because she was so exhausted and so miserable, maybe it was because she was forced to live so far beyond her capabilities, that she suddenly felt relieved that she was with a tough, macho, domineering—smart—man like him.

With Linc, she had a taste of how nice it would be to have someone stronger than she was to watch over her, to guide her someplace better than she could get to on her own. And maybe to take care of her, if only a little. So she wouldn't have to face the burden of life alone for once. At least for a while.

But that kind of dependence, that kind of weakness, was dangerous to indulge and lethal for someone like her. She was hungry for too much and had hungered too long to trust herself not to go crazy on a taste of something that could never lead to more. Or to anything permanent.

She was suddenly more miserable inside than she was outside. If she lived through this ordeal, her body would recover. It was the knowledge that her heart would never recover from this small taste of hope that made her feel so grim.

Maddie was so tired by the time they found a campsite along the stream, that she didn't care that Linc used her boot laces and the laces from her Nikes to tie together a crude frame of twigs for a rabbit snare.

He'd got a fire started and unfolded the blanket while Maddie braved a private trek into the trees. When she returned, she'd collapsed on the blanket and gone instantly to sleep. It couldn't have been much after four o'clock in the afternoon, but she slept hard. By the time Linc shook her awake, it was long past dark and getting late. It surprised her to see that the moon was out, and though it wasn't a full moon, it lit the valley they were in and extended the light of the campfire. Camping in the dense trees the night before must have kept her from being aware of it. It might also have been cloudy the night before. Something else she couldn't have seen through all those trees.

The smell of roasting rabbit was the only thing that could have persuaded her to crawl out of the blanket and make an effort to wash up in the stream so she could eat.

She squeezed her eyes shut so she wouldn't have to look at the small, nicely browned carcass on the crude spit. Her heart was heavy with guilt, but she was so hungry it was all she could do not to cry with relief when she had that first hesitant bite of food. Guilt overwhelmed her twice, and she almost couldn't make herself take a fourth and fifth bite. But then her empty stomach made it impossible to resist. By the time she finished the last scrap of meat, her raging hunger had been soothed, but the only thing she could think about was the poor little rabbit.

She wiped her greasy fingers on her filthy khaki slacks, too morose over the rabbit to care that she'd done such a disgusting thing. The red blouse and bush pants were ruined now anyway, which was why she'd changed back into them that morning after they'd dried overnight on the rope. She'd wanted to save her cleaner clothes for when they reached civilization. If they reached it.

It was Sunday night. Roz had said they'd only be in Aspen until Sunday afternoon. Whatever had happened when Maddie hadn't shown up had already occurred. Roz had surely written her off by now. Permanently.

Maddie's spirits were low. She stared into the fire, feeling tragic. Eating something and having a nap began to restore her, and she slowly began to feel less achy and exhausted. Their situation was truly grim. Before, she'd been so miserable she'd not been able to think about it. Now that she was so aware of how long they'd been on foot, it was all she could focus on. She was grateful when Linc distracted her.

"It's probably safe for you to wash up in the stream if you don't go too far. Wash those raw spots good so you can doctor them before you go to bed."

The idea of a bath lifted her spirits, but the effort it would take to get out her soap and her clean clothes made her slow to act. Besides, she remembered with complete clarity how cold the stream water was.

Eventually, she summoned the ambition to make herself move. She was stiff and her feet were so sore that she crawled to the net bag and her small suitcase. She might have considered crawling to a private spot a little upstream, but the grass was too deep and she couldn't forget the notion of snakes.

Maddie managed to get to her feet just as Linc got up to help her. She tried to ignore him. In spite of everything, whenever she looked across the fire at him she had to force herself not to stare. He hadn't shaved that day, and he had the black stubble of an outlaw.

So why did she suddenly find that appealing? Normally, she was repelled by men who didn't shave. They looked so dirty and disreputable. But on Linc, the dark stubble seemed to be just another indication of manhood in its highest form.

Frustrated with herself and her new preferences, she tried to summon the image of Beau. Handsome, *clean-shaven,* devil-may-care Beau. But no matter how hard she tried to form his picture in her mind, the only male face her brain could seem to locate was Linc's. And her eyes were locating him too often as it was.

Her bath was as traumatic and cold as she'd feared, but her poor swollen feet and sunburned skin felt wonderful in the chilly water. She managed to brush her teeth then wash her hair. Maddie didn't care at all that the shampoo bubbles might put a little pollution in the stream. She used one of the finest shampoos on the salon market, and if it ruined every stream and river that fed off this one, then perhaps someone would notice and trek into the mountains to find the source. And they'd be found.

The ridiculous thought amused her until she walked out of the water and realized that she had no towel to catch her hair in and nothing to dry off with. And the night air was cool.

Annoyed, she rummaged in the net bag and got out her second pair of clean jeans. She could use them as a towel and still have her other jeans to wear. Once she finished drying off, she got dressed. Forcing her bare feet into a pair of socks wasn't as hard as trying to put her boots on. Even without the laces in, the boots were too small for her swollen feet. She ended up hobbling back to the full light of the campfire in her socks.

Linc was still sitting by the fire, his extra clothes stacked beside him. When she went over to the blanket and collapsed as much as sat down, he got up. If you don't mind me usin' your soap, I'll go wash up.''

Her soft, "Of course, help yourself," made him reach for the bar of soap she'd set on top of the suitcase to dry. She grabbed the shampoo bottle she hadn't put away and held it toward him. "You can use this.''

Linc reached to take the bottle. "Much obliged." And then he walked away toward the spot where she'd bathed.

Maddie peered through the moonlight after him, checking to see how much he might have been able to see of her while she'd been taking her bath. He'd kept his back to the stream, but he might have glanced over his shoulder from time to time.

What she saw was Linc undressing. First he unbuttoned his shirt and peeled it off. The light wasn't good, but she could see enough to know what he was doing. For some perverse reason, she continued to watch, only able to force herself to look away when his movements suggested he was about to shuck his jeans.

She focused on searching through the small suitcase for the antibiotic cream and gauze patches. But her legs were so stiff that bending her knee to get her foot close enough to apply the cream made her leg cramp. After several frustrating tries, she finally gave up for a while, stretching her legs out in front of her while she waited for the spasms to die down.

She'd just leaned back on her hands to rest when she heard a stirring in the trees behind her. The sound froze her. A picture of the big brown bear flashed in her mind. A low snuffling sound and another rustle sent a wave of mindless terror through her heart.

*The bear had found them!*

# CHAPTER SIX

THE SCREAM SENT CHILLS over Linc's skin and he
surged up out of the water to look toward the campsite. Maddic was flying toward him across the grass,
screaming like a banshee. He automatically searched
the line of trees behind her and saw nothing.

He stepped out of the water, naked as the day he
was born, just in time for Maddie to fling herself at
him. He caught her reflexively and fell back a half
step when her small body collided with his.

"BEAR! Bear-bear-bear-bear!"

Catching her alarm, Linc glanced over her wet head
to look for the bear. He saw nothing this side of the
tree line, so he looked again, scanning for a dark
shape or some sign of movement. The moon lit everything with a soft glow, but even in the low light,
he could see nothing.

Meanwhile, Maddie was clinging to him like a
leech. She was shaking so wildly he could hear her
teeth chatter, and she was digging her nails so sharply
into his back that she must have broken the skin. He
released her to reach behind his waist to pry her sharp
little fingernails away.

She was surprisingly strong, and she refused to let
go easily. Finally, he got her loose and brought her
hands around to put between them. Then he remembered his nakedness.

He needn't have worried. Sniffling almost hysterically, she twisted her hands free, then grabbed his arm to whip around behind him to use his body as a shield. Her small hands gripped his waist to keep him in front of her, and every salon-groomed fingernail that hadn't been broken or torn off pinched into his skin like tiny pliers.

"For God's sake, woman, stop clawing me!" The gruff order somehow penetrated her hysteria, but he had to tear her hands from his waist and hold them a safe distance to free himself. "You probably took a few chunks of hide that time."

Maddie was further terrorized by his unconcern. Didn't he get it? Didn't he see it yet? The bear had found them!

"A *bear!* There's a bear!"

Linc's grip tightened on her wrists to keep her hands away from his skin. He turned his head to speak to her over his hard-muscled shoulder. "Where? Did you *see* the bear?"

The skeptical emphasis on the word "see" deflated some of her terror. She shifted and peered around him toward the campsite, frantically scanning everything she could see, particularly the trees directly behind the campsite.

"I asked if you *saw* a bear." He paused a moment as if he'd thought of something. "Or did you just hear somethin' movin' in the brush?"

The question sounded so sensible that she felt her face flush. She could see for herself that there were no bears in the moonlight. Her terror began to level off and slowly drained away, but she couldn't stop shaking.

"Answer me."

Maddie suddenly didn't want to answer him and shrank away from his back. His firm grip on her wrists kept her from getting more than a few measly inches. She hadn't *seen* a bear, she'd only heard a rustle and a breathing sound from some animal. There were millions of animals in the woods, jillions of small, harmless ones that could have made those noises. But she'd instantly concluded that she'd heard a bear. Now that there was no bear, she realized how foolish her hysteria had been.

She cleared her throat, delaying her confession a few more moments, loath to admit anything. Even she could hear the guilt that colored her voice when she forced out the words, "I…thought…there was a noise, something m-made a breathing sound. Kind of…a snuffle or growl, some odd sound—"

She cut herself off because she sounded like an idiot. A hysterical female who'd heard an odd sound and jumped to a huge conclusion. A craven little coward who ran away from imaginary danger. Her humiliation was so acute suddenly that she almost wished she *had* seen a bear. At least she could have died with some scrap of pride. There was no glory in cowardice.

Linc's rich chuckle nicked her pride. "You heard a *snuffle?*"

He tried out the word as if he'd never heard it before. "If a *snuffle* is anything like a sniffle, why didn't you just do something etiquette-like? Say, 'Bless you' and hand 'em a hankie?"

Maddie felt her temper ignite. "Very funny. And which comedian are you?"

"The naked one."

The low drawl sent a shock wave of revelation through her. Maddie had been looking up at what she could see of his profile over the top of his shoulder. Her chin dropped. Her gaze jerked down, then down, then down.

Though Linc was standing between her and the light of the campfire, there was plenty of moonlight. And it did a spectacular job of displaying the muscle definition and sinewy perfection of Lincoln Coryell's gorgeous male backside.

His gorgeous, *utterly bare,* male backside.

A little gurgle of dismay sounded in her throat. A gust of heat singed her sunburned cheeks. Every sensation she'd experienced when she'd flung herself into his arms and pressed herself against his back came to her in some sort of bizarre delayed reaction. *She'd felt everything!* The only way she could have been aware of more masculine details was if she'd been as naked as he.

Her soft, "Oh, my," was barely audible, but he could hear it.

"I reckon I'll take that as a compliment, Miz Maddie," he drawled, the lazy male smile in his voice hundred-proof Texas arrogance.

Maddie tried to pull out of his grip, but he was slow to release her. It was as if the testosterone-loaded beast was delaying her escape so she could get a better look. But she had perfect eyesight. It wasn't possible to get a better look than she'd got. Was still getting.

The moment he let go of her wrists, she ducked around him and hobbled through the grass toward the campfire, so stirred up inside—so turned on—she didn't know how she would stand it.

By the time Linc came strolling up from the stream to the campfire, Maddie had almost given up trying to apply the cream to the angry red sores on her feet. She literally couldn't bend her knees more than a couple of inches without setting off another leg cramp. The pain had distracted her from Linc.

But the moment he stepped into the circle of firelight, she realized the distraction had been temporary. She'd seen silly words in novels that read "her eyes swallowed him whole" and she'd giggled at them. The words weren't nearly so funny now that her eyes were literally devouring him. If eyes could inhale, that's what hers would have been doing with the masculine vision across the fire from her.

He was so big and rough-looking, broad-shouldered, narrow-hipped. Tough and male. Even his overlong dark hair, which was coal black in the low light, was thick and shiny and manly. His face was ruggedly handsome. An interesting face, with fascinating planes and angles, a strong jaw, a strong nose, and dark eyes that shone with intelligence and perception and just the smallest hint of desire.

Something had changed between them on the creek bank. Though in the grand scheme of things between men and women, it wasn't much, it—whatever *it* was—had happened.

The touching, the looking, the wild wanton feelings, those were the things that had affected her. What had affected him?

She'd been fully clothed and he didn't like her. Until it had dried, her hair had been wet and ropey;

she wore no makeup, and her face was bright with sunburn. She wore nothing to conceal her flaws or enhance her looks, nothing to lure him, not even perfume. Maddie knew the value of perfectly turned-out women, and right now she was about as far from perfect as it was possible to be.

She knew she had a good body, so maybe that was it. Who knew how much sex Lincoln Coryell was used to? It was certain he was more experienced than she. He'd got it right when he'd guessed she was a virgin. On the other hand, she was a female and she was conveniently close by.

Linc seemed to be having a fine time with every other aspect of tramping through the mountains. Maybe this masculine adventure had enhanced his appetite for other male pursuits. Maybe she was just part of the wilderness fun.

Maddie looked away from him, feeling reduced to the low status of a mere sex object. That's what a woman was when the man with her didn't like or respect or truly care for her. And why was that? Why was it only the woman who could be devalued in a male-female relationship, and not the man?

"I thought you were taking care of those feet," he said, his disapproval clear.

Good. Let him try to lord it over her so she could get her mind off male-female relationships of any kind and back on disliking him.

"Unfortunately, my feet are still connected to my legs," she groused.

Linc had started to crouch down on the other side of the fire from her, but at her answer, he paused and straightened to his full height. ''That your way of sayin' you can't reach your feet?''

The gleam of amusement in his eyes told her he'd guessed the answer. She sent him a cross look.

Linc walked around the fire to where she sat on the blanket. He hunkered down and wrapped the long fingers of one hand around her left ankle and carefully lifted it to inspect her foot.

The moment he touched her ankle, she felt the jolt of excitement. When he used the fingers of his other hand to help angle her foot into better light she had to bite her lip. The fiery shower of sensation that sizzled along every nerve in her body was stronger than the night before, and it was so wonderful, she could hardly stand it. After a day of agony, she was susceptible to anything that felt good, and Linc's hard, strong—warm—hands felt good.

''They look plenty red and raw, but you didn't rub them any bigger,'' he told her. ''Maybe need to use the cream morning and night.'' He set her foot down on the blanket and reached for the antibiotic tube and the gauze patches.

Maddie endured another erotic episode with her feet. It was so much more intense this time. Just like the night before, she sank back on the blanket and literally melted. The wonderful—dangerous—sensations came to an end all too soon as Linc finished and put her things back in the suitcase. He got up then and moved to a spot across the fire to crouch down. He broke a few of the long sticks in the pile of firewood and laid them in the fire.

Maddie struggled to sit up. The air was cold, but the fire felt good. The tense undercurrent between them made her restless. She was restless all over, nervous, agitated. The stark pleasure of Linc's touch had started it, and she was afraid she was slipping closer to emotional disaster.

"Any danger in you stoppin' that Valium cold turkey?"

The question came completely out of the blue. Her first reaction was anger, but her second was much more threatening. After taking care of her feet for a second time, the fact that he was also concerned about this hurt. He made her feel warm inside and just a little cared for. Lethal feelings. And she was such a sucker.

"There might be if I was addicted." Her words were stiff, but she was trembling inside.

"You sure?" The look he leveled on her was somber, and her agitation spiked high.

She was so rattled suddenly that the small defense slipped out. "It was a prescription for the weekend."

Appalled at herself, she rushed on to distract him. "If you'd bothered to read the whole label, you'd see there were only six pills." Somehow, her prickly statement got her in deeper.

One corner of his mouth quirked. "What was so awful about this weekend? Before we got started on our big camping trip, that is."

The faint humor softened her a little. What did it matter if she told anyone? Maybe she'd feel less tragic about her mother if she told someone something about it. Better yet, if she told Linc, maybe he'd make some remark that would make her angry, and anger would help her ignore the pain. Just like always.

"I was...going to meet my mother's new family."

She could tell the instant she said the words that he knew their significance. Her heart pounded suddenly with terror and regret. The soft look he was giving her choked her somehow and she felt her eyes fill with tears. Horrified at herself and humiliated, she struggled to turn and crawl on her hands and knees to her side of the blanket.

"How long's it been since you last saw your mother?" The low question froze her for a moment, before she recovered and tried desperately to smooth a wrinkle out of the blanket. Agitation made her too rough and she made it worse. Her eyes were swimming now and everything had blurred. Thank God he couldn't see her face.

"Maddie?" That one word—or rather the gentle way he said it—made a fat tear spill past her lash and spot the blanket. She sniffed hard in reaction and caught her breath midsniff because it sounded so loud and so obviously like she was crying.

Her rough, "What do you want?" sounded as bitchy as she could make it. She tried to sneak in another sniff—a short, quiet one—but it wasn't nearly short enough or quiet enough to go unheard.

"So it's been a long time." Something in his voice hinted that he already knew she hadn't seen her mother for years. More evidence that everyone in and around Coulter City gossiped about her behind her back.

She was rich now, could buy most anything she wanted, but she'd never been able to silence the rumor mill. She was seen as a tragic, odd, unwanted child who'd grown up and gotten rich and beautiful and hateful. A few people pitied her, most people didn't, but everyone was sickly sweet to her face because she had so much money and most of them had designs on it.

Just like when she was a child, she had no real value to anyone. Money had put a price tag on her, but no human value.

"You're makin' a mess of that, darlin'."

The low words rocked her and her heart gave a huge pained leap. Linc's voice had come from beside her as she fumbled with the blanket. She jerked her head in his direction and drew in a startled breath to see how close his face was to hers.

His voice dropped to a rasp. "I'll take care of it."

Her heart was pounding, shaking her whole body. It took everything she had to find a scrap of nastiness. "Suit yourself." She pushed herself up and sat back on her heels.

And immediately provoked an agonizing leg cramp. Her startled cry ended abruptly when she bit her lip and flung herself onto her side to straighten her leg. Her face blazed with shame because she'd actually cried out, but the tears that cascaded down her cheeks caused her a humiliation she hadn't felt in years.

Linc was over her in an instant, pushing her to her back and reaching for her ankle. She bit her lip harder when he lifted her leg, but the moment he dug the tips of his hard fingers into the knotted muscle she began to feel relief. He moved closer to her foot and raised her leg higher, using his other hand to grip her foot and press her toes toward the front of her ankle.

In seconds, the cramp began to relax. Linc pressed

deep into the muscle to force the knot to smooth out. His touch was magic, and the cramp eased completely until it was his fingers that caused the pain. As if he could feel that, he eased the pressure.

The pent-up breath she'd been holding leaked out of her on a wave of weakness. The tension seeped from her body as Linc kept her foot flexed and continued to work on the muscle.

That was when his touch began to affect her in another way. Strong, knowing fingers continued to smooth at the muscle. He slowly eased the pressure on her toes and released her foot to slide his hand up her ankle to join his other hand in the deep massage.

His touch was heaven. Firm and expert and so, so welcome. The deep hunger and wonderful sensual heat was starting again, and Maddie felt the first sharp points of another kind of pain.

She wished now that she'd tried to get to her feet to walk off the cramp. Linc wouldn't have been able to touch her like this. The terrible hunger and hope wouldn't have got started again, and she wouldn't be lying there in fresh agony over any of it.

Maddie didn't look at him, but kept her eyes stubbornly fixed on the moon-dimmed stars overhead.

"You're tensin' up," he drawled. "Relax, or you'll get it started again."

How could she relax? Her tension was a by-product of trying to resist what he made her feel, what he made her ache for. She was such a loser; it wasn't possible for her to ever win. She was in peril no matter what she did.

If she relaxed, she'd be more vulnerable to him than ever. But then, he'd let go of her and she'd lose the incredible pleasure of his touch. If she stayed tense, she'd have another excruciating leg cramp.

Finally, she made herself go limp. Prolonging Linc's reason to touch her would only make the loss worse later. Somehow, she had to get over this. She'd lived her whole life without Lincoln Coryell and his magic touch. She could damn well live the rest of it the same way.

Maddie tried to ignore the desolate feeling that swept coldly over her. At last, Linc set her foot down gently on the blanket, but he didn't take his hands off her leg. She could feel his gaze on her face, sensed the intensity of his scrutiny, but she didn't let herself look at him. She had to get him to stop touching her.

"Thank you." Her words were soft, but carried a trace of dismissal she hoped would put him off.

The remoteness she was trying so hard to achieve was suddenly blown away by his low, rough voice.

"I want to kiss you."

The shock of his words sent an earthquake of reaction through her. Her round gaze shot to his.

Linc's face was set in stone. It was hard to believe he'd spoken. If there was ever an expression that looked less romantically passionate and more unyielding, it was his. But his dark eyes were smoldering and she knew she'd heard right.

Her heart nearly beat her to death as he slowly moved his hands up her leg to her thighs. He came toward her on his knees, sliding his hands to her hips then to her waist.

Maddie stared, mesmerized as he slowly moved higher. Higher and closer until he shifted and nudged his knee between hers. The blatant sexuality of it sent an avalanche of desire through her.

And then his face was directly over hers. He'd braced a forearm beside her head. His right hand skimmed warmly up her side and was just now closing over her breast with agonizing care. His big body settled over hers.

Maddie could only watch as he leaned down and his chiseled lips descended those last few inches to hers. His fingers felt for the tip of her breast through the fabric of her blouse and bra, and when they found the goal and closed around the small sensitive spot, Maddie felt a hot, sensual explosion in the deepest part of her body.

Her swift, indrawn breath seemed loud in the firelight. Her eyes felt as round as saucers, and they moved in a short, erratic course from his eyes to his lips and back as he continued downward.

At the last second, when his lips came so close that she could feel their warmth, she panicked. His mouth barely touched hers and she abruptly turned her head, the light friction of sliding her mouth from beneath his sending equal parts of terror and excitement through her heart.

The wild thought, *I'm the only woman in these mountains!* was a desperate grab for some thread of self-preservation. Undeterred, his lips grazed the shell of her ear and her body jerked with pleasure. His warm breath was feather-light, but its effect on her was as strong as a hurricane.

Somehow she got her hands between them. His knee slid higher between her thighs in gentle retaliation. His lips toyed with her ear and fine tremors of pleasure and fear shook her.

It took everything she had to form the words in her mind and force them out to make him stop. "Get off." The fact that they lacked a scrap of indignation or true assertiveness dismayed her.

She tried to squirm from beneath him, but he slid his fingers into the hair at the back of her head and gently forced her face toward his. The fingers of his other hand lightly rolled and chafed the tip of her breast. Hot sharp sensations streaked through her like volley after volley of tiny pleasure-tipped arrows. His knee came all the way up and settled boldly against her.

At the same instant, his lips reclaimed hers and her fate was sealed. The initial touch of his mouth was tender and coaxing, and she lost her grasp on coherent thought.

His mouth slanted heavily over hers, the fresh pressure parting her lips. And then his tongue pushed in aggressively. The shock of the intimacy made her gasp and gave him deeper access. For several minutes, he touched and invaded and explored in a kiss so carnal she felt faint. It was impossible to resist anything now.

Maddie's hands slid up his chest and found their way around his neck. Without her hands between them, Linc eased more of his weight on her. Maddie couldn't help that she was kissing him back, pouring every ounce of passion and emotion she had into what she gave.

From there, things got wilder and more uninhibited. Linc flicked open the buttons of her blouse and his hand slid inside. She didn't know how his fingers got past her bra to her bare skin, and she didn't care. She was drowning in sensation and in the undreamed-of joy of being this close to another human being. Her hands were all over him, his arms, his shoulders, his face, in his hair.

The primitive urge to completely connect with Linc, to somehow absorb him and allow him to absorb her, made her whimper softly. She'd needed this, desperately needed this. She'd been starving for love her whole life, and suddenly Linc was offering everything she'd ever wanted from an unbelievable banquet of touches and tastes and violently sweet pleasures. Maddie's heart opened fully and completely to him, and the sure knowledge that he was offering her the riches of intimacy with him made her quiver with gratitude and joy.

And that was why she couldn't comprehend it when Linc's mouth slowly eased from hers. His fingers were still doing wonderful things to her breast, but even that stopped when he dragged his hand away and pressed his jaw against her cheek. They were both breathing so hard that neither of them could speak.

It was over. She knew in her heart that something was wrong and she was terrified of what would come now. Her body was still violently aroused, and she desperately tried to quiet it. Linc got his breath back before she did, and the moment she realized it, she felt the first poisonous stirring of dread.

How was it possible to have something so incredible happen with a man and it not be enough for him? She'd just had the most spectacular experience of her life yet she knew Linc was about to ruin it. Her dark flaw must be more awful than she'd thought.

*Please, Linc, don't spoil this.* She didn't realize she'd whispered the words until she felt the dull shock of hearing the sound of her own choked voice. Something inside her shrank in on itself. Oh, no, how could she have given herself away!

She pulled her arms from around him and pushed on his chest to signal she wanted him to release her. Instead, he lifted his head and looked down into her face. Maddie's eyes flinched from his and she made a restless move. His arms tightened around her.

"Where're you goin'?"

"Anywhere but here." Her voice was so hoarse it was almost inaudible. And she meant it. The last place she wanted to be was here with him. Not because she couldn't stand him, but because she couldn't stand to be so close when she knew it meant more to her than it could possibly mean to him.

Wendy Wilderness, the token bimbo on the male adventure in the mountains. Convenient and eager. Pathetically eager.

"I want to sleep now." The words came out stilted. Maddie kept her face turned slightly so she couldn't look him in the eye.

The warm crush of his body made it impossible for hers to calm down. It gave her ego a tiny boost that his body hadn't calmed either. She wasn't so virginal that she couldn't tell he was aroused.

Maddie made another restless move and Linc eased away. Because she was lying on her half of the blanket, she turned onto her side. She listened as Linc shifted and settled. The blanket dropped over her.

Linc lay close enough that the heat from his big
body scorched her back. But he didn't touch her.
The fact that he didn't made her heart feel heavier
than ever.

# CHAPTER SEVEN

MADDIE AWOKE SLOWLY that next morning. She felt more safe and content than she could ever recall. It was the novelty of those feelings that stirred her and brought her closer to wakefulness. She lingered in the haze, reveling in the sweet, rare emotions from some dream she must have had.

She snuggled deeper to cling to the warm feeling. That was the moment she realized where she was and what she was doing. *Her cheek was pillowed on Linc's chest.*

The small shock brought her fully awake and she jerked her head up. She was lying on her side facing him, but her left arm and leg were draped so far across his big body that she was practically lying on top of him. His left arm was wrapped around her and the fingers of his right hand loosely circled her left wrist.

When had this happened! She'd slept in the same blanket with Linc the first night, and as far as she knew, she'd never touched him, never turned toward him.

After their kiss last night, she'd planned to be cool and aloof with him this morning. But this was about as far from cool and aloof as it was possible to get short of complete intimacy. If he woke up now, it would be impossible to explain. She couldn't explain it to herself! She had to get off him.

Maddie watched his face closely, searching for any sign he might awaken. She started to pull her wrist from his loose grip, but the moment she did, his dark eyes opened and fixed on her rounded gaze.

She felt her cheeks go hot. Linc's wonderfully male mouth eased into an amused line, and Maddie scrambled to keep him from coming to the obvious conclusion.

"How dare you?" Her voice was husky from sleep, but the feminine growl was as close to genuine as she could make it. Indignation was a dandy distraction from what he must be thinking.

She tried to jerk her hand away, but Linc's fingers tightened instantly, as if he'd been expecting it. She tried to pull her leg off him, but it had somehow got caught in the blanket. All she could do was shift her right arm and get it under her to demonstrate her intention to move away. Linc thwarted that by flexing his arm to keep her close.

"Don't play the outraged virgin, Miz Maddie," he drawled.

*Especially after last night.* He hadn't said the words, but her brain filled in the blanks.

"What a colossal ego you must have," she tried next.

"Just keepin' you honest."

Mortified, Maddie tried to jerk out of his grip. He hesitated, then released her. In her haste to free her leg, she managed to tangle it tighter. Linc finally reached beneath the blanket, took hold of her thigh with breathtaking familiarity, and pulled her free. Maddie made a thoroughly awkward getaway and ended up on her hands and knees in the grass. Disgruntled, she faced forward to get up.

And came nose to nose with a small hairy face.

Her scream pierced the dawn. Linc grabbed her from behind and pulled her away from the hairy menace. She twisted to catch hold of Linc for protection, but couldn't take her eyes off the animal.

Startled by her scream, the small dog cowered back into the grass, trembling and terrified. The tension in Linc's hard body eased when he saw what it was and he pried her hands off him.

"Might be this is your bear."

Maddie allowed Linc to set her aside, and she continued to stare as he sat back on his heels and gave a soft whistle.

"Come on, fella," he coaxed. "She makes a lot of noise but she doesn't bite."

Maddie looked on, shocked at the sight of the small dog. Mostly black, it had brown around its face and on its feet. At least it looked black and brown. Its long hair was dirty and a couple of twigs and sticky leaves were tangled in the long strands.

It responded to the reassurance in Linc's low voice by whimpering and ducking its head. It half turned away, then turned back, as if it wasn't sure whether it wanted to stay or run. The obvious battle between longing and fear in the small creature got Maddie by the heart.

Linc continued to speak softly to the little dog, but the dog, however much it seemed to want to come close, kept a safe distance from them. Linc finally gave up when the animal showed signs of running away.

"Probably best to not push. We'll get some breakfast going, then see what it does."

Linc reached for his boots then, and gave every impression of completely ignoring the little dog. He stripped Maddie's laces out of her boots and set the boots beside her.

"Go on about your business so it can see we mean no harm. Probably best not to make any sudden moves or try to call it. By the time the fish are ready to eat, it'll be too hungry to stay away."

"How did it get out here?" Maddie suddenly had hope that the dog was a sign that they were near a road or highway or some other sign of civilization.

"Either got lost from its owner or was dumped out. A tame dog wouldn't survive very long out here. It's a wonder something wild hasn't had it for a snack."

Maddie looked up at him, hope blazing bright suddenly. "So we can't be far from help?"

Linc gave her a somber look. "Maybe. But if we're that close to other people, the dog might have found them before it found us." He turned for the stream bank, but called over his shoulder.

"If it gets close, don't let it bite you. No tellin' if its owner kept up with its shots."

Maddie was terrorized by the idea. After that, she kept the dog in sight at all times so she'd always know where it was. She didn't want it to suddenly attack her, as some sick animals could.

Every neurotic worry she'd ever had seemed to have been stirred up during this ordeal, and now something as normal and civilized as a small dog had added a new dimension to her fears. The fact that the nightmare kept continuing made her lose hope that they would ever find their way out or be found.

Linc had been careful not to get her hopes up, and she wondered if that meant he wasn't very confident about their eventual escape from the wilderness. The thought worried her. Today was the third day.

By the time she was finished with her morning walk in the woods and had changed into her dirty red blouse and bush pants for another grueling day, Linc had already caught two fish. She joined him on the stream bank to watch.

The dog shadowed her every move and sat several feet away on the bank. Even at a distance, Maddie could see the poor little thing shake. She could see the anxiety in its eyes—what she could see of its eyes through its ratty hair.

She decided that now was as good a time as any to ask Linc what he really thought of their chances.

"Do you think anyone's looking for us?"

Linc glanced her way briefly, but didn't answer right away. "If they know where to look," he finally said. "I can't be sure anyone heard my Mayday call, with the radio cuttin' out. Your mother probably called the authorities when you didn't show up."

Maddie's gaze fled his. She didn't want to admit to him that her mother was long gone from Aspen by now, and that there was absolutely no chance that Roz had called anyone.

"I've been lookin' for someone to fly over the area so I could shoot off a flare," he added.

"Surely someone's reported you missing," she said hopefully. Linc was the sort of person people missed.

Linc shook his head. "My trip was a when-you-get-the-time kinda thing. To a private airstrip. The weather was supposed to be clear all the way, so there's no flight plan to close by a certain time." He paused. "No one would know to call a search and rescue team."

Maddie felt hopeless. It would be unfair to let Linc think someone had notified the authorities about her when she knew otherwise.

"Then…I think that means no one's looking for us." Her quiet statement got his attention.

"What makes you say that?" The grim thread in his tone was the first hint that Linc wasn't perfectly thrilled to be lost in the wilderness.

Maddie took a quick nervous breath. "I mean that my mother invited me, but I didn't tell her when I was coming. Or if I was coming. Even if she called my staff, they probably don't know I took a flight with you."

She couldn't look at him now. "So, how much farther do you think it will be?" What she wanted was some sort of positive guess from him, something to hope for.

"We're smack in the middle of everything you saw when we were going down. That's a lot of miles."

His answer pressed her spirits downward. She covered it with sarcasm. "Thank you, Daniel Boone, for that optimistic press release."

He didn't answer her, and she didn't attempt further conversation. Eventually, he walked upstream to use the crude fishing line in another spot. By the time he came back to camp, he'd caught only four fish.

Maddie made herself watch him clean the fish.

Thank God he had a good knife, and even she had to admit he wielded it skillfully to fillet the meat. He threaded it all on a stick and set it across the two Y-shaped sticks he'd set up on either side of the fire. He tossed the heads, tails, and entrails into the stream. To avoid attracting predators, he told her. The little dog went back to the campsite with them, but kept its distance.

When the meat was done, Maddie had no better appetite for fish for breakfast than she had the day before, but for a different reason this morning. She was depressed. Today would be their third day in the mountains. If they didn't find some sign of a road or highway or other people, they'd have to sleep another night on some stream bank. If they didn't find their way out by tomorrow, it would be day four. Then five, then six. The days seemed to stretch out endlessly in a nightmare of exhaustion and hopelessness. It was only a matter of time before an animal attacked them or some disaster befell them.

Desperate to distract herself from her dismal thoughts, she looked on while Linc coaxed the little dog to him for a bite of meat. Because Maddie couldn't force herself to eat more than a couple of bites of her own meal, she gave the rest of her portion to the starving dog. She took care to pinch the meat first to check for any small bones not removed in Linc's filleting process, then fed the bits to the little animal.

But even though she was the one who gave the dog the most food, it favored Linc. That was evident the moment it finished her food, then went begging to Linc, who managed to pet it. A moment later, the dog bounded into his lap and stood shaking. Linc looked it over briefly, checking its feet, then announcing that it was a female.

Maddie looked on, touched by Linc's gentleness with the small animal, but let down because the dog favored him. She'd rarely been anyone's favorite, and that little failing apparently included dogs.

She must really be pathetic to be jealous of Linc's popularity with a dog. Unhappy with herself, she washed in the stream and brushed her teeth. They packed their things, put out the fire, then started out on another endless hike.

Today was worse than the first two days. They were walking through deep timber most of the day, detouring around dense underbrush, stepping over logs, constantly moving over small steep rises and dips that slowly began to feel taller and deeper. They found no grassy valleys. They'd angled far away from the stream because the undergrowth was thicker along the bank and much harder going. Maddie worried they'd lose their water source.

The little dog panted along behind Linc, ducking under the obstacles if she could or jumping over others. By noon, Maddie was certain the dog was tired. When she noticed it limping, she called ahead to Linc.

Linc walked back to where she and the dog had stopped and set down his duffel bag. He hunkered down to look the dog over.

''Looks like another female with sore feet,'' he said as he tucked the dog under his arm, then grabbed the handle of the duffel bag to stand and continue on. Maddie trailed along behind with her things, envying the dog its free ride.

She walked behind Linc all morning and well into the afternoon. By then, she was so exhausted that she was uncoordinated. Her spirits were desperately low. Every step they took to get free of these damned trees and mountains should have led them closer to the wonderful perks of advanced civilization. Instead, each step seemed to take them deeper into peril and deprivation.

They'd seen another bear. Thank God they'd seen it from a distance, but avoiding it had sent them higher against the side of a mountain. Which meant they'd climbed upward for what seemed like hours before they cut through the trees on a deer path that took them well beyond where they'd sighted the bear.

They'd taken periodic stops to rest but they'd eaten nothing. Maddie's stomach felt as shriveled as a raisin. She was so hungry that every food she'd ever disliked in her whole life managed to parade through her mind to taunt her. She was remorseful over any bite of food she'd ever left on her plate, and earnestly regretted the unnecessary deprivation of every diet she'd ever inflicted on herself.

That afternoon, a faint rumbling sound in the distance distracted her from starvation, and she was instantly excited. Maddie pictured some big semi on a nearby highway or a logging truck on a back road. She didn't know if any logging was done in that part of the mountains, but there were certainly enough trees to make this a lumberjack's paradise.

"Is that a semi? Could we be getting close to a road or highway?" She was ecstatic at the possibility.

Linc quelled her excitement with one word: "Thunder."

Maddie was furious with him for the blunt decree that dashed her hopes. Surely he was wrong. The small patches of blue sky she could see through the tops of the trees didn't show even a wisp of cloud. Thunder couldn't happen without clouds, so she clung to the hope that they were getting close to rescue. They seemed to be moving toward the sound, and she exulted in the notion that she was right and Linc was wrong. Within the next half hour, the distant rumble got closer and more distinct.

And Linc was right, it had been thunder. The daylight was starting to dim, and it was still late afternoon. Maddie glanced up a time or two, feeling her heart fall at the sight of the gray clouds that were now drifting into view.

Not long after, thunder shook the ground. Linc turned toward the stream and Maddie followed, grateful it was a downhill course.

Because they'd traveled all day on a path far from the stream, it seemed to take forever to find it again. With each step they took that didn't end on the stream bank, Maddie's worry about losing their only known water source increased.

The thunder boomed overhead and the first fat drops of water began to fall, but Linc kept moving through the trees. It seemed to take an eternity to find the stream, and by then the big raindrops were smaller and their rhythm had speeded up. Linc guided them to a small hill above the stream bank. By the time he got the roll of plastic out of his duffel bag, the rain was pelting them and they were rapidly getting soaked.

He slung the plastic over a low tree branch that

pointed toward the stream to form a quick, crude shelter that gave them a view of the water. Maddie got in with the little dog and dragged in her things. Linc ducked in with his duffel bag seconds later.

The moment they were all under the plastic, the rain began to pound down, making a low roar as it peppered the plastic. Linc had situated them above the stream bank on the hill to prevent the rainwater from running from higher ground into their makeshift tent.

Once again, Linc was proving himself smart and capable, a strong man fully equal to the challenge of the wilderness. Maddie felt completely inept. The independence she'd prided herself on was worthless out here.

Her wet clothes began to itch, giving her a new misery to endure. The thunder was deafening, and the plastic actually shivered with every boom. When the little dog began to whine, Maddie felt like whining with it. She reached down between her and Linc to comfort the animal, but Linc's hand was there first. The dog hopped onto his lap and snuggled against his lean middle. When Linc curved his arm around it, the dog stopped whining.

The dog's complete disinterest in her hurt. She'd made overtures to it today, feeding it her breakfast, speaking to it, lifting it over obstacles it was too small to jump over on its own. Linc hadn't given the animal a backward glance until its feet became too sore to walk.

Well, it figured. Someone else was always more valuable, someone else was always the favorite.

Maddie scolded herself for the petty thoughts, but felt her mood darken anyway.

"We'd a been smart if we'd grabbed a little firewood on the way down," Linc commented. With that, he passed the dog to her then leaned forward to duck out of their shelter.

The dog began to whimper the moment Linc handed her over, and Maddie had to hang on tight to prevent it from scampering out into the storm after him.

The fact that Linc was out there braving the lightning and a fresh soaking to find wood was another indication of his strong character. Maddie wasn't certain she'd be willing to do the same thing, though going all night without a fire wasn't something she wanted either. She was grateful for the way Linc was, but every good thing he did, every smart idea he came up with made her feel the weight of her inferiority. Why hadn't she thought of going back out into the storm to gather wood before it got too wet? She not only felt inferior, she felt small and shamefully self-centered.

By the time Linc returned with an armload of wood to put inside their dry shelter, he was drenched. Maddie leaned away and held the dog back as he peeled off his sodden shirt.

"Pardon me, Miz Maddie, but I need to strip these off." Linc leaned back to unsnap and unzip his pants and Maddie jerked her head to face away. There was absolutely no privacy and little enough room for him to change into dry clothes, but he got the job done. His arm brushed hers repeatedly, and it amazed her how easily excited she was by even his unintentional touch.

"You need to change outta that wet shirt yourself," he commented as he took the dog from her arms.

Maddie's gaze connected with his in the dim light beneath the plastic. She felt the jolt of the contact. There was just the smallest glimmer of male interest and desire, and her eyes shied from his. "I think I'll wait."

Maddie drew her knees closer and wrapped her arms around them. She'd already stiffened up from sitting, and the movement was painful. They both stayed silent as the rain continued to pound down. Eventually, it tapered off to an occasional tap-tap on the plastic as stray drops fell on the plastic from the tree branches overhead.

"I don't know that we're going to have enough dry firewood to both keep us warm tonight and get a fire hot enough to cook another rabbit. I'll leave the choice up to you."

Maddie was instantly and irrationally angry. She was frustrated and wet and terrified of facing another moment of wilderness deprivation. And now they were further reduced to choosing between two miseries: to be warm and dry while they starved—or to eat and freeze all night. There probably wasn't enough wood to fully cook a rabbit, or even a fish. Assuming they could catch any once the storm passed. *If* it passed. The rain had started up again.

"Oh, by all means, make the choice yourself, Jeremiah Johnson," she said, then cringed inwardly at her shrewish bad manners.

Linc didn't reply, which left Maddie's own words

to ring in her ears. God, she was a witch. An ungrateful little witch. And if she had any doubts about her abysmal faults, Linc leaned back to brace his elbows on the dry ground behind him and calmly began to chronicle them.

"I remember you back when I worked on your Grandma Chandler's ranch. You musta been all of fifteen when I first saw you out there. First thing you always did when that chauffeur dropped you off was to make a beeline for the newest colts. Most times, you were down to the barn or out to the pasture before you'd even changed your dress and your town shoes. Always saw you runnin' up to the house later to get your outdoor clothes before you'd go runnin' back out to the colts."

Linc paused for a while, as if the memory meant something to him. Maddie remembered those times with surprising clarity. It absolutely shocked her that anyone had paid attention to her back then, much less that *Linc* had and that he could retell those times in a way that suggested he was fond of the memories. It was all she could do not to look back at him to see if he was making fun of her in some way.

"You had a mouth full of hardware, and you were as long-legged and skinny as a new filly yourself. And you had a real gentle touch with those babies. As the year'd go on, they'd see that big black Caddie rollin' up the ranch road and they'd come runnin' to meet you at the fence." The faint smile she heard in his voice was not amusement as much as it was a sweet sort of sentiment. Her heart began to shake, and she was suddenly too restless to stand being under the tarp with him. But the rain had started up again, thwarting her escape, and her whole body went tense.

His low drawl went on lazily, but something in his tone warned her he was about to make a point. "In those days, you had a nice touch with everybody. You were so shy you blushed bright red whenever anybody said somethin' to you, but you were kind and sweet to everybody. Didn't seem to matter who it was, you were always polite and respectful."

*Not like you are now.* Linc didn't say the words, but she heard them clearly in the silence that followed. She was acutely uncomfortable.

"I was an awkward ugly child." The words were choked out of her, almost against her will. The admission shocked her, and she suddenly didn't know if she'd told him because she felt compelled to express her skepticism about the fondness he'd hinted at, or because she was trying to explain the difference between the pitifully needy child she had been and the witchy adult she'd become.

He ignored the statement. "That kid was sweet and special. I'll never understand why you threw her away." He paused, and his voice dropped lower. "She mighta been all braces and legs and straggly hair, but she was solid gold through and through. And worth at least a thousand of the woman who took her place."

His calm words were like a stake through her heart. Emotion welled up so forcefully and so fast that it was like a hot geyser. She gritted her teeth to hold it back.

"What did she ever get for being so good?" Maddie couldn't keep back the bitter demand. "The sweet never made up for the ugly." Her voice was rough with the pain she could barely hold back. "Not even—"

She abruptly cut herself off before she could say it all: *Not even to my mother and father.*

Linc's voice turned hard. "There's no such thing as an ugly child, Maddie. Bad parents with ugly hearts maybe, but no ugly kids."

Maddie couldn't help the compulsion to jerk around and look at him then. The utter sincerity in his dark eyes got her by the heart and squeezed mercilessly. She was profoundly moved by his terse declaration, and that was the precise moment that Madison St. John fell deeply and irrevocably in love.

But the pain of a lifetime, and the deepest fears she had, came roaring up. Linc was the last man she should love. He was too good for her, she didn't deserve him. Even if a miracle happened, and he could possibly feel something for her other than contempt, her strange dark flaw guaranteed she'd lose him. Just as she'd lost everyone else she'd ever loved.

As if he knew he'd managed to connect with her, he used the turmoil she was obviously in to drive his point home.

"I'm sorry for you, Maddie. Your parents didn't do right by you, and your grandma was as mean as a canker sore. They musta hurt you a lot, but none of it gives you the right to take it out on other people."

Maddie turned away as if she'd been slapped. The worst shame she'd ever felt came over her and went so deep that she felt nauseous. It suddenly didn't matter that it was raining hard again. She couldn't stand to hear another word, her heart couldn't bear to listen to another hard truth.

She practically flung herself into the storm and slid down the bank to the stream. Then she was running along the flat part of the bank until she found a path and could run up the bank farther down from their small shelter. She was too weak to run far, and caught herself against a narrow tree trunk. She gripped the tree and cried, grieving for the sad child she'd been and so ashamed of the person she'd become that she sank to her knees and sobbed.

# CHAPTER EIGHT

LINC MADE NO ATTEMPT to stop Maddie. He knew his words had hit her hard. She'd need some time to herself. He hadn't made up the story about the sweet shy kid she'd been. He hadn't needed to. It was because of that sweet shy kid that he'd dared to confront her. Probably why he'd let her fly with him to Colorado in the first place.

Madison St. John had potential. If for no other reason than he'd known firsthand the kind of kid she'd been and what she'd had to grow up with. And she was right. She hadn't got anything for being good; not much of the tragedy in her life had been improved by her sweetness. Now she was mad at the world, a professional victim who demanded compensation and made everyone pay for the sins of a few.

He wasn't the one who'd done her wrong, and neither were most of the people she ran roughshod over. If there was any chance for her, any hope, this little adventure in the wilderness might be the thing that brought her closer to it. The little despot needed to be forced out of her narrow kingdom, needed to correct her thinking and her attitude toward the world.

Deep down, he knew the biggest challenge for her would be to correct her thinking about herself—about both the injured kid she still carried around inside her, and the angry off-with-their-heads queen she'd become.

Madison St. John had a conscience; she knew she was doing wrong. She was so guilty about the things she'd done that she was neurotic with it. The unhappiness in her adult life was her own making, and only she could change it.

Linc was powerfully attracted to her, fascinated by her complexity, and touched by her vulnerability. He'd felt no guilt, had no hesitation about confronting her, about pushing her to face herself.

He hoped she'd decide to be the good person she was capable of being, because there was a lot about Maddie that was still worth taking a chance on.

Maddie trudged back wearily to the shelter long after dark, guided by the warm firelight she could see through the trees. She hovered well away from the circle of light and watched Linc. He'd built the fire just outside the overhang of plastic. He'd also managed to stretch the plastic farther past either side of the branch to form more of a canopy than a tent. Thunder rumbled in the distance, but it was moving away from them. Weak moonlight filtered through the treetops, so it might not rain again tonight.

Maddie was thoroughly exhausted. She'd sobbed herself silly and had suffered such a profound agony of the soul that she'd felt close to dying from it. She still felt deeply ashamed of herself. Regret was all she could think about and she was so hollow inside that her skin felt like a thin paper shell. She wanted to do something to fix every bad thing she'd ever done, but she wasn't sure how. She wasn't sure anyone would let her.

The rebellious part of her rejected the idea that

Lincoln Coryell, with his folksy cowboy simplicity, could possibly figure her out and deliver such a sharp reproach.

The part of her that was honest knew absolutely that he'd been brilliantly astute about her. Painfully so.

God, how he must despise her! *She mighta been all braces and legs and straggly hair, but she was solid gold through and through. And worth at least a thousand of the woman who took her place.* He couldn't have made his opinion of her clearer.

The fact that he must have liked and approved of her once was the only thing that gave her hope. It was literally the only thing that gave her the courage to go back to that shelter and face him.

"You might as well come on in and get into some dry clothes." His low voice carried to the dark shadows where she lingered, exposing her. "It's gettin' late."

How late, she couldn't guess. Her body felt like midnight. She was freezing in the night air and her teeth were chattering convulsively. By the time she could force herself toward the fire and the shelter, she was trembling with fear and cold.

She couldn't look at Linc when she got there. The little dog yipped a greeting, but she was too dispirited to respond. She pried her muddied boots off and left them outside the shelter to duck down and go inside.

Maddie was too cold to worry about changing her clothes with Linc there. Though he turned his back to give her what privacy he could, the fact that she changed every scrap of wet clothes for dry ones within two feet of him made her feel peculiar inside.

Thrilled, terrified, and excited. Maybe even a little turned on. That was when she knew she was demented.

*There's no such thing as an ugly child, Maddie. Bad parents with ugly hearts maybe, but no ugly kids.* The man who believed that was a man to be demented about. Linc was also a good man, a kind man in spite of his tough talk, a man who could be trusted. Something in Maddie relaxed, something gloomy and lost in her warmed just a little. A faint spark of hope glowed bright, but she fought it down.

Hope was still dangerous, and it might always be. Longing was positively lethal, but the longing she felt for Linc was too powerful a compulsion to fight. The best she could hope for was to endure it in silence. Alone.

Maddie didn't bother to doctor her feet. When Linc offered, she quietly refused, and she was relieved when he didn't insist.

For the third night, she lay down beside him on her side of the blanket, facing away from him. But this time, when he tossed the edge of the blanket over her, his arm came around her waist from behind and he pulled her back snugly against him.

It was like suddenly being pressed against the side of a hot furnace. Maddie stiffened, doing her best to resist. She made a restless move to ease away, but his hard arm flexed and pulled her tighter against him. A flash fire of desire swept her.

''Go to sleep, darlin'.'' Linc's Texas drawl was a husky rasp. Maddie's heart grabbed the endearment and hoarded it close.

Maybe Linc didn't quite hate her, maybe he was

willing to give her a chance. She had no idea what to do with a chance, but somehow she'd figure it out.

The little dog climbed carefully onto their feet and dropped its small weight down with a weary thump. It shifted, and Maddie heard a small growling sigh of contentment.

The warmth of Linc's big body finally made her stop shivering. It was heaven to be held against him, to feel the weight of his arm around her and his warm breath stirring her hair.

Maddie stared into the fire thinking about her life—thinking about Caitlin—until her eyelids grew too heavy to keep open.

"Mind your manners."

Linc's order was low and brusque, and gave Maddie a start. Her eyelids fluttered against the early light. The dog gave a little whine, and Linc shushed it. Assured it wasn't her he was ordering about, Maddie snuggled deeper in the blanket, so tired that she fell back to sleep instantly.

Sometime later, she felt Linc's hand on her shoulder. "Breakfast's near done, Miz Maddie."

*Miz Maddie.* Respectful, but distant. Very distant. She felt the heavy emptiness inside her before she remembered the events of the night before. And when she remembered, all she wanted to do was pull the blanket over her head and sleep for weeks.

But Linc expected her to get up, and it relieved a part of her guilt to be able to meet such a small and simple expectation.

Maddie sat up and leaned over stiffly to reach for her boots. Most of the mud had been scraped off or knocked off, because they were free of the mud that had crusted them the night before. Her gaze flitted past the rabbit meat roasting over the fire to locate Linc. He was crouched next to one side of the cook fire, turning the meat. The dog was sitting on the other side across from him watching every move he made.

Cleaning off her muddy boots was a kind act, just as putting her laces back into her boots that first morning had been a kind act. Then, she'd been angry because kind gestures from people who didn't like her were easily mistaken for something they weren't. This morning she didn't feel like trying to figure out.

"T-thank you for cleaning off my boots." She'd said it hesitantly, then was deeply ashamed because she wasn't used to expressing gratitude. But it had sounded okay, and that relieved her a little.

Linc turned his head and his dark eyes fixed on hers. "Feelin' better?" The penetrating look he gave her went straight through her brain. She felt as if he could read her mind. He'd certainly read everything else about her that she thought had been shielded from the world. His ability made her a little wary of him.

"I'm fine."

He allowed the small evasion. But what else could she have said? *I feel terrible because I've been such a horrid person? I'm fine* was the truth. She'd lived through last night and she was still alive this morning. She had to be fine to have done that.

"Fresh outta fish this morning," he commented, and though he didn't smile, there was a glint of humor in his dark eyes. "We'll probably have to mud-wrestle Skeeter for our share of the rabbit."

As if the dog already recognized her name, she yipped and sat back on her haunches to put her muddy front paws in the air to beg. The pose was adorable, startling a small laugh out of Maddie.

"Figgered she needed to be called somethin'," Linc told her. "She's about the size of a Texas mosquito, and in case you haven't found out for yourself already, she's got fleas."

The pronouncement didn't faze Maddie. Yesterday, she would have gone off the deep end over the mention of fleas. It might very well have been the end of the world. It would at least have been one more misery to feel sorry for herself about.

Now she thought about the misery fleabites must be causing the little dog, who could do nothing better than scratch or bite itself for relief.

"Do you think a bath with something in my case might help get rid of them?" she asked.

Linc's gaze shifted briefly to the small suitcase. "No tellin'. Water might be too cold for her when we don't have an easy way to get her dry right away. Dogs like her are a little fragile. Maybe if we hit a long spot of hot sun, we could try it."

Maddie couldn't get over how easy the small talk was between them. Her first instinct was to discourage it, but that would mean being nasty. And she didn't have the heart to be nasty. In fact, the way she felt now, she wasn't sure if she could ever be nasty again.

But the easy talk was somehow threatening. The trick would be to end it in some inoffensive way. Maddie looked down and reached for her boots. She forced the stiffened leather onto her feet, then got up.

She was a little less creaky and sore this morning,

and that lifted her low spirits a bit. "Time for that walk." The faint smile she offered felt unnatural, but she did it anyway.

As she walked carefully across the incline in the upstream direction, she watched for a break in the trees above the stream that would lead to privacy. A little huff-huff sound behind her made her glance back to see Skeeter trotting along after her as if the tiny dog was going along for protection. Or maybe female companionship. The notion made Maddie smile, and eased some of the heavy guilt on her heart.

Skeeter was a shameless little beggar at breakfast. She used her small dark eyes—somehow the hair that constantly fell into them parted just enough to show her expressions—to give them pitiful looks. And she certainly wasn't above adding a long, husky little whine that seemed to say, "Oh, I'm sooo starved, can't you spare this tiny baby dog another bite?" when they both determined not to look at her. Skeeter ended up with more meat in her belly than they did.

Packing up their meager belongings and putting out the fire had become so routine that they cleared it up quickly and started out.

Maddie tried to ignore the hopelessness of another endless walk. Today, she was determined to find something about it to enjoy. After last night's rain, the earth smelled rich, and the trees were a deep, vibrant emerald. There seemed to be more deer paths with fewer obstacles on their journey today. Now that her legs had recovered somewhat from the unaccustomed exercise, they felt stronger and surer on the path.

Maddie still felt the deep, hollow weight of regret, but there was also a strange peace mixed in with it. She had the odd feeling that there was nothing to fight about, no reason to be so vigilantly on guard to protect herself. It took her most of the morning to realize that she was no longer tense and anxiety-ridden.

Losing her last chance with her mother still made her sad, but she didn't feel like clinging to the hurt anymore. Instead, she thought about the people she'd hurt with her arrogance and sharp words, with her snobbery and peevishness.

She thought about her chauffeur, John, her cook, Esmarelda, and her maid, Charlene. It was a wonder John hadn't driven her car off a cliff, Esmarelda hadn't fed her poison mushrooms, and Charlene hadn't smothered her with a dust rag! In her fear of letting anyone close, of allowing anyone to take advantage of her, Maddie had been curt and superior and aloof with each of them.

Now she felt so ashamed of her bad behavior that she spent a good share of the morning trying to think of how to apologize, how to make it up to them. That's when she began to think of everyone else she'd bullied these last years. The woman who colored her hair the exact shade Maddie decreed, the harried clerk at Neiman Marcus who could never seem to please her, the solicitous waiter at her table in her favorite restaurant. It mortified her now that she'd thought hefty tips gave her license to be rude and demanding and impossible to please. The number of people she needed to make up to seemed to number in the thousands.

And then she thought of Caitlin.

Caitlin. Her blood cousin, her oldest, dearest friend. Maddie thought about Beau and how he'd died, and suddenly, she knew absolutely that Caitlin, however much she'd disliked Beau and had felt jealous of him, would never have done anything to jeopardize his life.

If Caitlin said she hadn't been able to save him from drowning in that flash flood, then it was the gospel truth. Caitlin had never lied, not even to get herself out of hot water with her father and stepmother. She couldn't have lied about Beau's death.

How much had Caitlin been wounded by Maddie's abandonment and her hateful refusal to believe in her? It was entirely possible that Maddie would have to face the fact that there were some things she'd done that could never be fixed, some bridges so burned that no trace of them remained to so much as mark the way back.

And it could never be the same for Caitlin. Maddie had betrayed her in a way that no one else could have because they'd been so close. Maddie should have been her cousin's staunchest defender and most dedicated ally. The fact that she'd behaved like Caitlin's worst enemy was something neither of them would ever get over.

The hollow weight inside her now weighed a ton. It was unbearable and she suddenly didn't have the energy to put one foot in front of the other on the path.

By early afternoon, she was only dimly aware when Linc stopped them for a rest. Her heart was in turmoil over Caitlin and the enormity of it all. She found a spot to sit down and gingerly lowered herself to brace her back against a tree trunk. She was so downcast that she stared blindly at the base of a tree trunk several feet away.

"Somethin' eatin' you?"

Linc had sat down against a tree trunk to her left and he'd stretched out his long legs. Skeeter had dropped down beside his booted feet and lowered her head to her paws. Her small dark eyes flitted from him to Maddie then back as she endeavored to keep track of both of them.

Maddie glanced his way briefly. The blunt perception in his eyes made her gaze shy guiltily away. But he was the one who'd yanked the royal carpet from beneath her feet and forced her to face up to what she'd done and what she'd become. Though she was experiencing some of the most profound emotional anguish of her life, she was surprisingly grateful to him. Perhaps she could confide in him now, even if she couldn't bring herself to tell him everything.

"Do you think I can ever make up for the things I've done?" She'd meant to find a more roundabout way of asking that, but in the end, the question came out in the straightforward way that made her anxiety increase.

Linc looked away from her and was silent so long that her anxiety became unbearable. When she reached the point where she began to think it might be better for everyone if she was never found, he spoke.

"I reckon that depends on whether you're sorry because you did them wrong and want to make it right because they deserve it, or whether you're only sorry because you want to get into their good graces to make yourself feel better or be more popular."

Maddie felt her eyes sting madly. If it was possible for her to be more disappointed in herself, his words got the job done. She was more miserable than ever. It was hard for her to face it.

"I can't say that I don't want to feel better," she confessed, her voice catching before she went bravely on. "I need to do something to cope with this guilt. But I honestly and truly want to apologize and do something to make up for things."

She stopped to bite her lip viciously to hold back the tears and repress the huge tide of emotion that made it difficult to speak. Her voice was hoarse with the effort.

"However anyone takes it, I owe it to them. Even if they can never accept my apologies, or me, I have to do it. I can't be the person I was another moment, and I can't just go back and behave differently without acknowledging the bad things I've done."

She couldn't help the short, deep sniff that she drew in to keep the tears back. She exhaled on a harsh little laugh that was anything but an expression of amusement. "I may not know who I am anymore, I may not even be sure how to act with all of them now, but I have to do something. I hope I don't make too big a mess of it."

She stared down at her hands, not really caring that they were filthy or that her perfectly manicured fingernails were blunt and most of the nail polish chipped off. What she looked like meant nothing. What she did and what she was inside were the only things that truly counted.

Linc's voice carried a calm tone of reason and simple wisdom. "You've got better instincts than you realize, Maddie. Your heart's in the right place."

Maddie exhaled a nervous puff of air and made herself glance over at him. She tried a smile that felt weak and uncertain. "There are some who'd say I don't have a heart at all, or that it's no bigger than a mean little dry cinder."

Linc's lips curved. "You'll have to get yourself a CAT scan or one of those MRIs and carry the proof around with you."

Maddie smiled then and dropped her head back against the tree trunk to stare up into the leafy branches overhead. Linc's teasing advice eased the turmoil inside her and lightened her spirits.

Skeeter's sudden growl got their attention. The little dog was on her feet, staring off down the left of the path they were on, her small body bristling. Her high-pitched growl trembled with almost comic ferocity, but there was no doubt that she was alerting them to danger.

Maddie felt a trickle of alarm. "What do you think it is?" Her brain pictured another bear or some other large predator.

Linc took it calmly. "She did that this morning with the rabbit and at least a half-dozen ground squirrels before you were awake."

Maddie's worry eased. Considering Skeeter's tiny size, just about anything was a threat.

But Skeeter continued growling periodically as they gathered their things and went on. Maddie could tell that whatever Linc had told her to keep her from worrying, he was more alert now, more vigilant as he scanned the dense woods around them.

After a while, everyone's tension eased to a more normal level of watchfulness. Skeeter continued to growl from time to time, but Maddie wasn't certain whether the small dog had given up on convincing them of some unseen menace, or if there truly was nothing out there bigger than some harmless animal.

Linc turned toward the stream soon after. It couldn't have been later than three in the afternoon, but he'd decided that they needed to make camp early. They'd both heard a faint rumble of thunder like the day before, and though the sun still blazed brightly through breaks in the tree tops, neither of them relished facing another downpour unprepared.

Linc ordered Skeeter to stay with Maddie while he went off to gather firewood. Maddie kicked some dry leaves together in a spot that looked good for a fire on a small rise next to the stream bank. Skeeter stayed with her, but paced around the campsite, alternately bristling and growling.

Without Linc's comforting presence, Maddie began to feel edgy. Because they were completely vulnerable to any wild animal, she scanned the area and spied a four-foot length of dead tree branch that was as big around as her upper arm. Maddie walked over to pick up the stout piece of wood and gripped it in both hands to take an experimental swing at a nearby tree trunk.

The sharp whack jolted her hands, but the wood was solid and if she had to wield it for any serious reason, it would make a reasonable club.

She was just hefting it for another experimental swing through the air when Skeeter went wild, growl-

ing and yapping and tearing off away from the campsite in the direction Linc had gone.

Maddie hesitated, but Skeeter's ferocity clearly
meant she was after something. She gripped her new-
found club and followed. A few feet up the rise,
Skeeter switched direction and was barking wildly off
to the right. The horrifying squeal Skeeter let out then
made her heart jump.

Tiny Skeeter was no match for any animal larger
than a rabbit, however fierce she sounded. Maddie
hurried through the timber in the direction she'd heard
the pained squeal and the wild barking started up
again.

Though Maddie was thoroughly terrorized and pre-
pared for something the size of Godzilla, she was still
shocked when she burst into a small clearing and saw
the giant golden cat on an outcropping of rock.

The outcropping wasn't more than two feet off the
ground, but the cat was crouched there, glaring down
at little Skeeter with murder in its eyes.

Maddie froze with the club in her hands, too pet-
rified to move. The big cat shifted on the rock and
swung a lethal paw in Skeeter's direction. Though the
arc of the swing barely came within five feet of where
Skeeter stood yapping wildly, the small dog yelped
as if it had been shredded to bits by the cat's long
claws.

Skeeter backed farther away, digging her small
paws into the earth to scrape back little clots of dirt
and leaves like some miniature bull about to charge.

"S-skeeter!" Maddie tried to call the dog to her in
the wild hope that they could just back away and

leave the cat alone, but Skeeter obeyed her only minimally.

Skeeter backed up about three yards then stopped. At almost the same moment, the big cat slunk down and its big body flowed elegantly down the face of the outcropping to follow. It stayed on higher ground than Skeeter, but it kept coming toward the noisy little dog, slowly, menacingly, its mouth open as it gave a series of throaty hisses.

Skeeter backed up and up, but the big cat moved in slow motion to stay with her. Maddie tried to back away, but Skeeter stopped, and as if she were protecting Maddie, began barking so hard and so fiercely that she went hoarse.

The big cat crouched and Maddie suddenly knew it was about to spring. Skeeter was too stubborn to leave and the cat was too attracted to the small hairy prey to find something else to do.

Maddie watched in terrorized disbelief as the big cat's muscles bunched under its golden coat. It would spring now, and Skeeter would be dead the moment the cat landed. In the next half second, Maddie lunged forward screaming and waving her club in the air.

She was marginally aware that the big cat gave a start and crouched lower. She was completely aware the moment the cat's eyes zeroed in on her and narrowed to hateful slits.

But it had stopped bunching its muscles to pounce. Its posture was defensive—Maddie prayed that's what it was—and she pushed her advantage of surprise and moved jerkily forward. She screamed her lungs out, shouting threats and orders as she swung her club and tried to appear more fierce than the cougar.

It all happened in a few wild heartbeats of time. So quickly that Maddie thought at first that she'd hallucinated. One moment the cat was crouching defensively, its ears so flat against his wide golden head that they were invisible. The next, it streaked to the side, disappearing into the trees so suddenly and with such a mercurial flow of motion that it seemed to vanish before her eyes.

Maddie stopped and stood poised like a statue in a ballplayer's pose. Skeeter went silent, her small body rigid as if she was listening to the sound of the cat's retreat to make sure it had really gone. Linc's voice boomed from behind them both.

"What the *hell* were you thinkin', lady?"

Linc's obvious fury was a new shock and Maddie turned toward him in an odd daze. He was stalking toward her, his face flushed with anger, his eyes blazing. "Didn't you hear me yell at you? That cat could have had you in two seconds and dragged you off before you could twitch!"

A strange little smile came over her lips. She felt so odd suddenly, but her heart was bursting with euphoria. "I scared him," she said, so amazed she had to repeat the words. "*I* scared *him*."

Linc reached her then and came to an abrupt halt. He loomed over her, so furious that he was like a column of weathered granite. Unafraid, Maddie's strange little smile widened to a grin.

And then she fainted.

# CHAPTER NINE

MADDIE WOKE UP to an impressive recitation of swearwords. Her eyes fluttered open and she realized she was lying half on the ground, half in Linc's arms.

Linc's face was harsh and his eyes were dark with turbulence as he glared down at her. It shocked her to realize she must have fainted.

"You little fool."

Linc's gruff declaration hurt her feelings, but the feel of his big palm on her cheek was soothing. Memory came swimming back, and she caught her breath.

"The cat—"

"You're damned lucky it wasn't hungry."

Maddie frowned, thinking that an odd remark. "How do you know it wasn't hungry?"

"There's a fresh deer carcass over the hill. What's left of it."

Maddie stirred, trying to sit up. Linc allowed it but kept an arm around her. The movement made her dizzy and she lifted a hand to her forehead.

"Then I wasn't hallucinating? There really was a cougar?"

"Hell, yes, it was a cougar," he roared. "What did you think it was?"

Maddie quivered and turned her head to eye Linc warily. His fury surprised her. He was always so cool, so in control. To see him like this unsettled her.

"I knew it was a cougar," she told him, "it's just

that everything happened so fast. One moment it's there and about to kill Skeeter, and the next it vanishes.''

Linc gave a curt nod. ''It could just as easily have grabbed you by the throat.''

Maddie shook her head. ''I couldn't stand by and just let it kill the dog.''

Linc hands slid up to grip her shoulders and give her a little shake. ''The dog wasn't where she was supposed to be. It would have been sad for the cat to get her, but she put herself in harm's way. The minute you decided to charge in, it was your life that was in jeopardy. And for what? If that cat had gone after you—''

Linc cut himself off and swore again. To her surprise, he leaned toward her, gave her a swift, hard kiss, then stood, lifting her with him. ''Can you walk?''

Maddie nodded, though her head was whirling from the unexpected kiss and her knees were shaky.

''Then let's get our gear and move on. And we'll make a leash for the little troublemaker so she doesn't stir up any other dangerous animals.''

Linc practically dragged her back to the campsite. Skeeter trotted along after them, her eager huff-huff-huff keeping pace with them.

Skeeter whined at the indignity of the leash. Linc had decided their rope was too heavy for such a tiny dog, so he got out a package of Maddie's panty hose to fashion a lightweight leash.

By the time they started out, Skeeter had settled down to an occasional whine. They hadn't gotten far before the little dog started limping again, so Linc tucked her under his arm.

They walked on for an hour, and Maddie was relieved that the thunder they could hear in the distance didn't seem to get much louder. Finally, just as Linc was about to turn back toward the stream, he stopped on the path.

"Hear that?"

Maddie stopped beside him and listened. She couldn't hear anything unusual above the twitter of birds and the occasional rustle of tree leaves in the faint breeze. She hadn't heard the faint rumble of thunder for quite some time. Linc stepped into the lead, continuing along the path, but at a faster pace.

Maddie caught his urgency, and she felt an answering trickle of excitement. What had he heard? She called a quick, "What was it?" but Linc gave her a noncommittal, "Let's wait and see," that sent her excitement soaring.

Though they'd been gradually going downhill, the path began to angle sharply downward. The last few feet near the bottom were steep. Maddie's feet slid several times, though she managed to stay upright. Linc reached the bottom first, then waited for her to join him. On her way down, Maddie caught tantalizing glimpses of a grassy meadow between breaks in the trees. By the time she caught up with Linc, the meadow was in full view.

The meadow was part of a valley. The creek they'd been following—she assumed it was the same one—cut through the length of it. At the far end of the valley, above the valley floor against the foothill of another mountain, a section of paved road was visible.

A white car suddenly appeared from the right and sped along the brief section of highway they could see before it disappeared. A minivan coming from the opposite direction drove into sight at a slower speed.

Maddie couldn't contain her excitement and turned to Linc to grab his arm. ''I don't believe it—we did it!'' Maddie released his arm and flung herself against him for a jubilant hug. Linc stiffened a moment, then hugged her back. His arms tightened fiercely around her, nearly cutting off her breath. Maddie felt the significance of the hard hug, but she didn't understand it. When she drew back to look up at him, he bent his head and kissed her. The kiss was brief and unsatisfying, but she interpreted it as the emotional release of finally escaping the woods.

Linc's rugged face softened into a wide smile. His dark eyes were gleaming. ''Let's see if someone'll give us a lift.''

Maddie suddenly didn't have an ache in her body, and she hurried with him across the grassy expanse to the rocky hill below the highway, so excited she could barely keep herself at a brisk walk.

Linc put Skeeter in the duffel bag, then slung the long strap over his shoulder. The hill was so steep that they practically crawled up. The little dog caught their excitement and yipped her encouragement all the way to the top while her head and front legs hung precariously outside the bag.

Once they were on the pavement, another minivan of vacationers came along. Linc waved them down.

Their trek through the wilderness ended rapidly then. The small family made room for their gear and gave them a lift to a ranger's station. After Linc gave them a report, they were given a ride to Colorado Springs. They checked into two connecting rooms at a motel, and Linc left for the airport to make the necessary report there.

Maddie showered, ordered room service, then shared a meal with Skeeter. They both fell into exhausted sleep before Linc got back to the motel. Maddie was awakened the next morning by the small, excited dog yipping madly at the connecting door.

Something had happened during their night-long separation. Maddie knew it the moment she saw Linc's face. He was distant with her this morning. He offered to take Skeeter for a walk, but he didn't join her when she ordered a room service breakfast.

He'd been gone for several minutes before the phone in her room rang. Linc was calling to tell her he'd taken Skeeter down the block to a veterinarian for an exam and a series of shots. Since they didn't know Skeeter's history, he'd considered that a necessity. When they got back to Maddie's room over an hour later, Skeeter had been bathed and groomed and was tethered to a respectable leather leash. The pink bow in her hair was adorable.

Linc's mouth was twisted wryly. "Felt strange walking such a sissy dog down the street." Skeeter tried to jump on the bed to show off, but was too small to make it. Linc scooped her up and tossed her on, and she tramped over the rumpled bedclothes looking for a soft spot to sit.

"So she's a Yorkshire terrier?"

Linc nodded. "Cleaned up nice, didn't she? They figured her about a year old. Hard to believe there was a high-class pedigree under all that moppy, dirty hair. I left my name and phone number at the vet's in case someone reports her missing.''

The room went silent after that. Silent and awkward. Everything had happened so fast. First the cougar, then finding the highway, then their sudden return to civilization. Whatever sense of comfort and near companionship they'd forged together in the wilderness was all but gone. They'd lived through a plane crash and most of four days of difficult isolation together, but suddenly they were strangers again.

Three nights ago, Linc had kissed her into oblivion, and she'd slept rolled in a blanket with him for three nights. Two nights ago, he'd confronted her and forced her to face the person she'd become, forever changing her attitude toward the world and affecting how she would behave for the rest of her life.

But as he stood looking at her across half the distance of a motel room, things felt as wary and uneasy between them as if they'd never met before that morning. Maddie's eyes began to sting.

How had it all slipped away? The past few days had been some of the most traumatic and wonderful of her life. Now suddenly, they were over. And not just over, but so insignificant to Linc that he seemed to have assigned them almost no personal importance. The fragile emotional bond she'd thought had formed between them suddenly seemed to have been nothing more than the result of an overactive imagination.

In spite of everything it had meant to her, it'd been nothing more than a wilderness adventure to Linc. A test of manhood that, from the vital look about him, had been invigorating and satisfying, but in the end, was nothing near the very personal, life-changing trial it had been for her.

Maddie had fallen in love with him. Deeply in love. It seemed that such a monumental event should be shared, should affect both equally. But it was painfully clear to her now that she'd been the only one affected, the only one who could have fallen in love. Because she'd been so awful there'd been nothing for Linc to fall in love with. Hadn't she known all along that love, when it came, would only happen for her?

Oh, God, what was she going to do? She felt raw inside, restless and unbelievably hurt. Pride wouldn't allow her to show it, so she tried mightily for the same emotional distance that Linc had accomplished so effortlessly.

"So, how do you plan to get back to Texas?" she asked. This might be a good test. If she figured into his plans, she could take it as a hopeful sign. If not...

"Thought I'd rent a helicopter and a pilot and try to locate the crash. If I can, I'll have your luggage sent home."

He couldn't have made things clearer than that, but he added a polite, "Will you fly back?"

Maddie felt herself break a little inside. "I'm not sure if I can even think about getting on another plane."

Linc gave her a steady look. "You probably ought to make yourself. Unless you plan to drive everywhere you travel from now on."

Maddie knew he was right, but she felt faintly sick at the thought. She glanced over at Skeeter, whose small dark eyes shifted between the two of them as if she was following their conversation.

"If I take Skeeter home with me, I don't want to think about her shut in some cargo hold." She glanced back at Linc. "Unless you're planning to take her with you?"

Linc shook his head. "You can take her if you like. Only dogs that fit my lifestyle are hounds or cow dogs. I could make an exception for her, but if you want to give her a good home, go ahead."

"D-did the vet think her owner will show up?" Maddie hated that her voice cracked on the word. She hoped Linc would take that to mean she was attached to Skeeter instead of heartbroken over him.

"He didn't think there was much chance. Said some vacationer probably lost track of her. Considering the area she was lost in, the owner probably gave up on finding her days ago."

Maddie nodded. "You'll let me know if anyone contacts you about her?" she asked, aching already for any excuse to hear from him again even if it meant bad news about Skeeter. On the other hand, if Skeeter had a family somewhere...

"Will do."

Maddie gripped her hands together nervously in front of her. This was it. The polite goodbye.

"Well, I suppose I need to call for a rental car."

"I'll take care of the cost of the car and the room," he told her.

Maddie stiffened. "I managed to carry my handbag all the way back to civilization. I have credit cards and plenty of money."

"I owe you. For the inconvenience of the crash. I'll take care of the cost of your troubles."

Maddie shook her head. "There's no reason for

that. You refused to let me pay you, so it wasn't a hired flight. Besides, I forced you to take me with you."

Linc started to say, "You oughta know by now—" but Maddie cut him off.

"I won't hear of it," she said quickly, slipping a little into the imperious tone she'd used with such success these last years. She cringed inwardly, privately appalled that the ability still came so easily. Maybe she didn't have enough good character to follow through with the change in her life after all. The thought made her feel even more tragic and downhearted.

"Whatever you say, Miz Maddie." Linc's drawl was cool and Maddie felt the chill of it to her soul.

*Please, Linc, don't hate me again. I truly have changed, I promise. The moment you walk out of this room so I can fall apart in private, I promise to never again be the bitch I was before. Please know it someday. Please care a little to find out.*

"Well, that's it, then," she said, squeezing her hands together so hard that her fingers ached. "I'll say goodbye now, so we can both get started."

Linc was staring at her, and it was another long, penetrating look that seemed to see between every brain cell in her skull. She gave him a tight smile and hoped he would never know how devastated she was to rush him off and go back to her lonely desperate life with no hope of joy.

Skeeter, as if she'd sensed this was goodbye, launched herself off the bed and bounded over to Linc. He crouched down to pet her and give her a gentle rub. "See ya 'round, Skeeter. Mind your manners with Miz Maddie."

Linc set the little dog aside and stood up. He said nothing to Maddie. Just looked at her solemnly as he reached up to pinch the brim of his Stetson in a polite cowboy salute. And then he was gone.

Skeeter stood staring at the closed door, cocking her little head to the side and letting out a growling whine of dismay. Maddie's knees gave out and she dropped down on the edge of the bed, her heart aching so hard that she felt like whining with the dog.

Maddie drove back to Texas. It was a long, quiet, exhausting ride. Skeeter was just as quiet as she was, and nearly the whole trip, she lay next to Maddie with her little head hanging over the seat as if she was too depressed to live another minute.

They arrived in Coulter City after 10 p.m. three nights later and Maddie carried Skeeter directly upstairs to bed. Charlene rushed from the servant's quarters at the back of the mansion when she heard Maddie come in, but the little maid disappeared instantly when Maddie quietly told her she wasn't needed.

She and Skeeter slept in that next morning until after eleven. When they got up, Skeeter seemed more restored to normal, and eagerly inspected Maddie's suite of rooms. Maddie could barely move, but put on a robe and took Skeeter downstairs to let her out on the front lawn.

She was as silent as possible to avoid having to face her staff before she was ready. Skeeter was too eager to get back into the house to linger over her morning walk, so the two of them stole back up the stairs.

When they came downstairs later, Maddie had showered and done her hair. She let Skeeter go to explore the house. Maddie hadn't bothered with much makeup, and she'd dressed simply in a pair of crisp gray slacks and a white cotton blouse.

Instead of walking into the dining room where she knew the long glossy table was already set for her lunch, she went into the kitchen where John, Esmarelda and Charlene would be having their meal.

The three of them came to their feet the moment she walked into the room. Maddie felt a guilty pang over the surprise and concern on their faces.

"I was wondering if after you finish your lunch, you'd all mind meeting me in the libra—no, the parlor," she said, hoping the less formal choice of room would set them more at ease. "I have something I need to say to the three of you that I hope—" Maddie cut herself off. "If you wouldn't mind," she added, acutely uncomfortable.

She couldn't miss the quick worried glances that shot between the three as they nodded and murmured "Yes, miss."

As she turned to walk out of the kitchen, Esmarelda called after her, "Would you like your lunch served now, Miss?"

Maddie glanced back. "No thank you, Esmarelda. I'm not hungry right now."

Maddie was relieved to escape the kitchen, but the wait in the parlor was excruciating. It pained her when her staff showed up much sooner than she'd expected, as if they'd rushed through their meal or hadn't finished it at all. What a shrew she must have been for these three people to be that worried about the possibility of displeasing her.

And they were worried. She could see it in their eyes as they filed quietly into the parlor and assembled in a neat line in the center of the floor. Skeeter trotted in after them and joined the lineup.

"Please," she started, then gestured toward the sofa and the chairs that flanked it, "Please sit down and...please make yourselves comfortable."

Again there was the exchange of glances between the three, but they each took a seat and looked at her expectantly. Maddie cleared her throat, so choked she was afraid she couldn't get the words out.

"I wanted to speak to the three of you first, because I think it's the three of you I've been the rudest and most ungracious to."

Caitlin Bodine Duvall had heard about her cousin's plane crash. She'd dialed the mansion in town several times, but hung up before she could punch in the final number.

All of Coulter City was abuzz with fresh gossip about Madison St. John. So much so that the stories had made it to the Broken B.

The general opinion was that Madison must have thought she was going to die and had experienced some sort of religious conversion. Either that or she'd got knocked on the head and couldn't remember who she was. She'd been lost with Lincoln Coryell in the mountains for most of four days. Because Linc was known as a tough, no-nonsense hombre, most were speculating that he'd tamed the town shrew. How he might have accomplished that feat was cause for ribald speculation.

Poor Maddie. If she'd changed back into a nice person, people might not be willing to accept it now. Or her. Maddie had always had a hard time fitting in. She'd be horrified if she'd heard everything Caitlin had.

It was Beau's death that had devastated Maddie and made her bitter toward life. If Maddie truly had changed, Caitlin hoped it meant that she'd finally gotten over the terrible way Beau had died. Even if Maddie could never bring herself to believe Caitlin's side of things or to forgive her, if she'd been able to find some peace about it, Caitlin would be glad at least for that.

Caitlin stared out the big windows of the den at the Broken B, but didn't turn when she heard Reno come in.

Her husband of one month stopped and slid his arms around her from behind. He bent his head and pressed his lean cheek against hers. Caitlin lifted her hands to his and gripped them gently.

"When d'you think we ought to get down to Duvall Ranch?"

Reno had mentioned yesterday that they needed to get back to his ranch near San Antonio. They'd decided to keep both ranches going for now, dividing their time between them so Caitlin could have time to consider whether she really wanted to sell the Broken B to Lincoln Coryell or not.

"Can we wait a couple more days?" she asked.

Reno moved his cheek against hers and tightened his arms. They'd talked about Maddie, and Caitlin had confessed her secret hope: that Maddie had changed, and that if she had, maybe she could finally accept the truth about how Beau had died. And if she could accept it, maybe she'd want to heal the rift between them.

"You've had enough heartache over Beau and Maddie," he said quietly. "Don't open yourself up for more, darlin'. Please."

Caitlin made a restless move and Reno loosened his arms. She turned toward him and slipped her hands around his waist to hold him close. "Two more days, Reno."

Reno looked out the window over Caitlin's dark head. "Two days." If Madison St. John didn't come through for Caitlin...

He pressed a kiss into his wife's soft hair and didn't let himself finish the thought.

The hardest thing for Maddie was not the apologies she made to the people she'd treated so poorly. The most she was apologizing for was her rude, curt words, her impatience, and her superior, impossible-to-please attitude.

The hardest thing was working up the courage to see Caitlin. Somehow apologies seemed trite when what you had to apologize for was the monumental sin of betrayal.

Because she *had* betrayed Caitlin. Betrayed their deep friendship, betrayed their love for each other, betrayed their blood kinship. Maddie might never know how deeply she'd injured her cousin, and she wasn't certain she could live with herself if she knew it all.

Caitlin had accepted her unconditionally when they were children. She'd offered her friendship and her loyalty and it would never have been possible for Caitlin to turn her back on Maddie as Maddie had done to her.

Of all people, Maddie knew precisely how sharp and deep the pain of rejection and abandonment could go, how crippling it could be. And yet she'd done it to Caitlin more suddenly and completely than it had ever been done to her.

When the guilt of what she'd done finally outweighed her fear of facing Caitlin, Maddie got into her car and drove to the Broken B.

Maddie rode the bay gelding Reno had saddled for her. Caitlin was out riding, and Reno didn't expect her back for at least a couple more hours. Now that Maddie had worked up enough courage to go to the ranch and apologize to Caitlin, she was afraid she'd lose her nerve if she had to wait.

Reno had been reserved with her. She'd felt his sharp scrutiny, seen the judgment in his eyes. But he'd accommodated her request to borrow a horse so she could ride out to meet Caitlin. He'd selected and saddled the animal himself. But the final glance he'd leveled on her had been harsh with warning. Maddie's gaze had fled his and guilt had nearly choked her.

It hurt to know how deeply she was disliked and mistrusted, but it hurt worse to think about the hurt she'd caused others. She deserved to be mistrusted and despised, and wished with all her heart that she'd done things differently, that she hadn't been so selfish and self-centered and mean. That she hadn't turned her back on Caitlin.

It had been ages since she'd been on a horse, but it wasn't long before the bay felt natural under her. Caitlin was the better horsewoman. Caitlin had been better at everything. Maddie had never minded that, because she'd admired Cait so much.

She didn't realize until she saw the long curving canyon that cut over that part of the ranch that she was close to the place where Beau had been killed. She remembered the area, remembered how fierce flash floods could be as they thundered through the canyon. She'd known the exact spot where Beau had been killed because she'd heard where it happened and could picture it in her mind.

Now she rode toward the sweeping bend where the flood water would hit hardest. Water traveled in a straight line, and when it hit a spot where it was blocked or forced to turn, the water pounded violently against it. The large chunk of sod that had been torn away was even larger than Caitlin had described, but there'd been five years of other floods since Beau's death. Five years for the water to resist the curve and sweep more chunks of it away.

Maddie pulled her horse to a halt and dismounted to walk to the edge. Beau's face was dim in her mind. It surprised her to realize that when she looked at the spot where he'd fallen in that she didn't think of how he'd died so much as how terrible it must have been for Caitlin to witness it. Watching the bank fall away, then making the mad, fruitless scramble to save Beau's life.

Maddie heard the clatter of hooves as a horse

walked down the rise behind her. She stiffened, then glanced over her shoulder.

Caitlin, her dark hair drawn back in a braid, rode toward her. The quintessential Texas cattlewoman from the crown of her black Stetson to the blunt-tipped rowels of her spurs, Caitlin Duvall was the feminine counterpart to the cowboy mystique. Strong, capable, and savvy, she was a match for any man or animal. Maddie was never more aware than at that moment how frivolous and pointless her own life had been, never been more ashamed for what she'd done. At the same time, the pride she felt in Caitlin was enormous.

Caitlin's eyes didn't leave hers. Her gaze was direct, but if she was searching Maddie's face or trying to read her intent, it wasn't obvious. She pulled her black gelding to a halt a few feet from where Maddie stood. Only then did Caitlin break eye contact. Her gaze shifted away from Maddie's to focus on the canyon.

"I'm glad you're all right," Caitlin said softly.

Maddie's eyes stung with gratitude and a tiny glimmer of relief. Caitlin was giving her an opening. Maddie took a quick breath before she could lose her nerve.

"There's no excuse for what I did to you, Caitlin. I betrayed your friendship and turned my back on you during the most traumatic time of your life. I'll never forgive myself for that, and I'll never forget." Maddie had to stop, because her emotions were overwhelming and she was determined not to cry. She didn't want to give Cait the impression that she was looking for sympathy. Caitlin was too soft-hearted not to be persuaded by tears, and Maddie didn't want that.

"I don't expect to have your friendship again, I don't deserve it. The only thing I hope is that you'll realize how profoundly sorry I am, and that somehow it gives you comfort."

Maddie's voice broke on the word and she hastily cleared her throat, though nothing could dislodge the lump that was choking her.

"You're the most honest, honorable woman I know. I'll regret it for the rest of my life that I didn't stand up for you then, that I turned against you." Maddie paused again, and looked away from Caitlin's sad profile to stare into the distance. "If I could go back to that day and do it over..."

Maddie went silent then and bit her lip. There was no going back. It had all been done, the cruel words had all been said, the wounds had been inflicted. There would always be terrible scars. The horrible finality of it still awed and traumatized her.

The squeak of saddle leather and the ching of a spur made her glance toward Caitlin. Caitlin had dismounted. The ching ching of the two steps Cait took toward her made Maddie's body go so tense that she thought she would shatter.

"I love you, cousin." Caitlin reached for her and caught her in a tight hug.

Maddie caught her breath, then jerked her hands up and hesitantly put them around Caitlin. She could barely get the words out. "I love you, too."

Reno was watching as Caitlin and Maddie walked to the house from the new stable, their arms around each other's waists, their laughter drifting toward him.

From the looks of their red eyes and noses, they'd bawled themselves silly, but the aura of happiness and companionship around them was as strong and vibrant as the two of them as they spoke animatedly to each other and shared another laugh.

A feeling of peace spread through Reno's chest and went deep into his heart. The past was finally in the past where it belonged, and the future glowed ahead of them all like burnished gold.

Maddie and Caitlin spent most of that evening and the whole next day catching up. By the time Caitlin and Reno left for his San Antonio ranch, the two cousins were closer than ever.

Maddie had confided a few of the details of the crash and the time she'd spent with Linc in the mountains, but she couldn't bring herself to confide her feelings for Linc. Caitlin didn't press, but Maddie had seen the speculation in her eyes.

The next day, a man from Linc's LC Ranch brought Maddie's luggage to the mansion.

"Took 'em a couple days to spot the crash. The Boss had other business to take care of and only got home yesterday," the ranch hand told her.

That was enough for Maddie. Linc could have brought her luggage himself. The fact that he'd sent one of his employees to do it let her know that he wasn't interested in seeing her again.

She'd gotten over a lot in her life—she was getting used to the fact that she'd never hear from Roz—and she'd get over Linc. After all, they'd only been lost together for three nights and most of four days. Add to that another night and a morning at the motel. Hardly enough time to justify her secret hope that there might be a chance for something more between them in the future.

The fact that she'd been foolish enough to somehow hope for it anyway caused her more than a little anguish.

Though Maddie made a sincere effort to apologize to everyone she could think of these last weeks, she was still terrified of how people would react to her. Without the armor of arrogance, she felt painfully vulnerable, and she was even more aware of how sensitive she was to being accepted.

At eighteen, her improving looks and instant wealth had given her access to anything or anyone she wanted, so she'd never truly had to cope with relationships in any more than a superficial way. With Beau dead and Caitlin estranged from her, she'd avoided all but the most shallow relationships and had accumulated a handful of rich, frivolous acquaintances who were almost as shallow and frivolous as she'd been.

Consequently, they were taken aback by the change in her. Maddie was no longer a good shopping companion because she wasn't obsessed to have the latest fashions. Art had become something that hung on a wall or sat on a table, not an acquisition to advertise status or good breeding. And now that Maddie treated food servers, shop clerks and salon personnel with courtesy, she wasn't nearly as entertaining. Maddie knew it was just a matter of time before they drifted away. Which was fine, since she doubted they'd fit into the new life she meant to have.

Now that she was ashamed of the self-indulgent lifestyle she'd led, Maddie looked into a handful of local charities that were as interested in the donation of her time as they were in her money. Though the organizers seemed a bit wary of her, they'd welcomed her interest and Maddie felt she'd made a good start on doing something useful with her life.

# CHAPTER TEN

THE BIG FALL BARBECUE at the Broken B was well attended. Reno and Caitlin were hosting the event, but Maddie privately considered it a sort of official coming-out party for the improved Madison St. John.

She'd chosen to wear a pastel multistripe cotton sundress with a fitted bodice that tied on the shoulders, nipped in at the waist, then flared femininely to her knees. The pink sandals she wore matched one of the narrow pink stripes in the sundress. Though the dress wasn't expensive or the supreme height of fashion, it was simple and attractive. With a minimum of makeup, she had a fresh, girl-next-door look that she hoped made her seem more down-to-earth and approachable.

The barbecue guests were a lively cross section of Texas society and culture that included everyone from Broken B ranch hands, neighbors and townspeople, to several of Reno's business associates and acquaintances in the ranching and oil business. Maddie hadn't asked if Linc had been invited, but he was a neighbor and she knew he was interested in buying the Broken B. She assumed he'd show up, but she tried her best not to actively watch for him.

Maddie was uncertain of her place in the diverse crowd. Reno and Caitlin helped her ease her way in, introducing her to everyone she hadn't already met. The number of people was a little overwhelming, but

Maddie soon relaxed. To her surprise, she found herself the focus of several of the single men there, from ranch hands to oil men.

When Lincoln Coryell arrived just after six, Maddie made no special effort to gravitate in his direction and, to her secret dismay, he made no effort toward her. The barbecue was served soon after and they were separated in the informal buffet line by at least fifty other guests. Later, they seated themselves at the two tables that were furthest apart.

Maddie couldn't help that her gaze strayed frequently in Linc's direction. Every unmarried woman in their part of Texas seemed to have ended up in Linc's general vicinity, and Maddie was forced to watch as several of them found an excuse to pass by him and say hello.

It surprised her and soothed her ego when several of the single men asked her for a dance later on, but she was noncommittal, pleading an inability to dance well. Which was completely true, since she'd almost never dated and hadn't had much practice with dancing. She was amazed by the number of offers for lessons, and managed to fend them off with a pleasant, "We'll see."

But if she'd kept herself from any real commitments in the hope that Linc would ask her to dance, she was sorely disappointed. For the first two dances, which Maddie sat out, Linc chose two different partners. Maddie understood then how things would be, so she began accepting dance partners.

An hour into the dance, just after the country band had started a ballad, someone tapped her partner on the shoulder and cut in. Suddenly, she was passed into Linc's arms. Shock made her hesitate.

She'd danced with several men already, but the difference with Linc was immediate. He was taller than most of the other men, and his natural dominance was evident even on the dance floor. Somehow he was surer of himself than the others, and he was definitely a better dancer.

And a more bold dancer, she realized instantly. Linc pulled her against him right away, sliding his hand down her lower back to press her against him with a sensual familiarity that made her heart race. The heat of his body radiated through their clothes and scorched her. He bent his head and his lips came close to her ear.

Maddie stared blindly at his lean jaw, overwhelmed by him. She could barely breathe. Her legs were unsteady, but the slow rhythm of the dance made it easy to cover that.

"Looks like you're real popular tonight, Miz Maddie." Linc's voice was a lazy drawl, but she heard the faint edge behind his choice of words. Her first impression was jealousy, but she dismissed the idea as wishful thinking.

Linc couldn't care less how she spent her time or with whom. He'd made no move to stake out any territory with her, no effort to see her these past weeks or to so much as phone to see how little Skeeter was doing.

"You've certainly been busy keeping the ladies happy," she returned stiffly. They were at odds somehow, and she knew her comeback wouldn't help.

"I hear you've made some changes."

Whatever Maddie had heard in his voice before wasn't evident now. She realized then that his mention of the changes she'd made was a tiny reproof for her remark to him about keeping the ladies happy. It demonstrated that his comment on her popularity and the one about the changes were related to each other and had nothing to do with any hint of jealousy. Maddie felt her cheeks heat.

"I've made an effort," she told him quietly.

Maddie glanced away from the handsome line of his jaw to focus her gaze at the top of his shoulder. She couldn't breathe properly and her heart was racing irregularly. It was torture to be held against him. She had to do something to distract herself.

"Caitlin says you're interested in buying the Broken B."

Linc didn't answer right away. Instead, he maneuvered her to the edge of the dance floor.

"I'm not interested in talkin' business tonight."

The roughness in his voice suggested wonderful, impossible things to Maddie. With any other man, the fact that he'd taken her to a more secluded spot on the dance floor and refused to talk business might be an indication that he was considering a kiss.

But this was Linc and he was dancing with her, not one of the other single women who were probably more to his liking than she was. She'd already misread too much tonight for this to mean what she thought it did—what she was suddenly starved for it to mean. Disappointment made her heart clench. She couldn't cope with the sweet pleasure and secret pain of being in his arms another moment.

Maddie stopped dancing and pulled back. "Excuse

me, I need something to drink.'' Relying on the element of surprise, she made a quick move to slip out of his arms, then walked with as much dignity as she could across the dance floor, weaving around the other couples. She stopped at the refreshment table and helped herself to a glass of lemonade. The icy drink slaked her thirst and helped steady her nerves.

As if her brief contact with Linc's big body had magnetized hers, she knew the instant he caught up with her. She was shaking, but downed the rest of the lemonade. Because she sensed he was stepping up to the table beside her, she set the glass down and turned in the opposite direction as if she were unaware of his presence.

Linc caught her arm before she could take a step. Maddie froze. She could either jerk away from him and risk that someone would see, or stand where she was and hear whatever he would say.

"I was wonderin' if I could give you a ride home."

Whatever she'd expected him to say, it wasn't that. "It's not even dark yet. Besides, I brought my own car."

"I'll get someone to drive it home for you." Linc ignored her remark about the early hour and eased closer. Maddie felt a tremor go through her. Why was he suddenly taking over?

"I'm not ready to leave," she tried next. Why hadn't she just refused to let him drive her home? And why would he want to drive her home anyway? And why so early? Besides, it was going to be a late night and Caitlin had invited her to stay over. Oh God, she was no good at this.

She felt his warm breath gust over her cheek as he

leaned close. "All right, Miz Maddie. I reckon you oughtta have one night to enjoy bein' one of the most sought-after heiresses in Texas. Just don't pick out one of those lovesick cowpokes or oil men and get somethin' started."

Linc released her arm. By the time she could glance back at him, he'd turned and was walking away from her. He was waylaid almost instantly by a tall brunette. He leaned toward the woman to hear what she said to him, then slipped his arm around her narrow waist and whirled her onto the dance floor. Maddie was left to stare after him, thoroughly shocked by what he'd said to her and completely confused about what he'd meant by it.

And then she felt the slow, hot burn of rising temper.

It had been *weeks* since they'd parted ways at that Colorado Springs motel room. Since then, Linc hadn't tried to see her, he hadn't even called. Now he'd shown up at her cousin's barbecue, ignored her until an hour into the dance, then suddenly had a stray whim to dance with her.

And then not to just dance with her, but to suddenly take over. To take her away from the dance early and take her home for God knew what reason. Then, when she'd refused to leave, he'd magnanimously "allowed" her to stay, but had ordered her not to get something started with any of the other men there.

The colossal gall of the man set her off. She was always the one who had to wait until someone else found time in their busy schedule to bother with her. Maddie's charismatic father had chosen to vanish completely from her life, Roz spared her five minute phone conversations every year or eighteen months, and her grandmother had often refused to allow Maddie to share a meal with her in the dining room because Maddie was too "colorless" to be an interesting dinner companion. But the moment the old woman wanted her to do some slavish task, Maddie couldn't come running quickly enough to satisfy the old witch.

Even Beau had been in sole control of when she got to see him. Caitlin had been the only person in her life not on her payroll who'd been available any time of the day or night, who'd included Maddie in her life as often as possible and still did.

Lincoln Coryell, whatever was going on in his domineering Texas brain, had turned out to be just another in a long line of people who were only occasionally in the mood for her company. When Maddie put that together, she was at first hurt, then quietly furious.

She had a new life and she was never going to wait around for some arrogant, domineering cowboy tycoon to find time in his busy schedule to crook his finger at her or give a whistle.

Even more riled by the image of that in her mind, Maddie looked for Linc on the dance floor, located him, then started in his direction. She walked boldly up to him and the brunette, tapped the brunette on the shoulder, then gave the woman a sweet smile when she glared at Maddie for the intrusion.

"Excuse me, darlin'," she drawled as she pulled Linc's hand from the woman's waist and nudged her aside. She flashed the startled brunette another smile. "You can have him right back, I promise."

Maddie dragged Linc three steps away before she stopped and placed his hand at her waist. She pushed her fingers into the palm of his hand and growled, *"Dance,* cowboy."

Maddie took the first dance step. Linc hesitated, then apparently decided to let her have her way because he took over. The condescension Maddie read into that small act made her even more angry. Linc's handsome mouth quirked indulgently as he led them in the dance, but his dark eyes were alive with amusement.

Which further infuriated Maddie. "I appreciate you taking care of me in the mountains and getting me safely out," she told him, "but if you'd made any assumptions about something between us later on, the time to act on them was weeks ago. As for who I choose to get something started with tonight, that's *my* business."

The line of Linc's mouth had gone level, but Maddie was too worked up to care. They'd both stopped dancing. "And no matter how it might have gone between us when we got back to Texas, I'd never give you absolute power over me, or allow you to dictate how I live my life." She was compelled to repeat herself: "I'll start anything I please with any man here."

Her declaration delivered, Maddie pulled back and took Linc's big hand off her waist to tow him toward his prior dance partner. Anger gave her surprising strength, but then, they were only three steps from the other woman, so it didn't matter that the most she might be doing was forcing Linc to extend his arm. Maddie grabbed the brunette's manicured fingers and placed them in Linc's. She forced a smile. "Here you go, sweetie, he's *all yours.*"

Maddie turned and stalked off the dance floor, not stopping until she'd crossed the patio and let herself into the kitchen by the back door.

Skeeter had been standing guard under the kitchen table, and when Maddie came in, she burst into a series of excited yips and scrambled across the tile, her tiny feet working hard to get purchase on the smooth floor.

Maddie leaned down to snatch her up, then hugged her close beneath her chin to walk through the house to the front door. Since Caitlin was almost as crazy as she was over the little dog, she'd included Skeeter in her invitation for Maddie to spend the night.

It'd been a while since Skeeter had been outside for a walk, so Maddie grabbed the leash on the hall table, snapped it on Skeeter's collar and let herself out the front door. She carried the tiny dog around to the side of the house where there'd be no guests and set her down. Skeeter went right to the end of the leash, then wandered around in the grass.

Maddie was shaking in the aftermath of her blowup. She'd pledged to change her ways, and she'd been quite good these past weeks. But she'd lost her temper with Linc. On the other hand, she'd needed to make a point with just the right impact to make it effective. Maddie couldn't imagine doing that if she'd simply taken Linc aside and explained things to him in some roundabout namby-pamby way.

Skeeter was ready to go in soon, obviously favoring the indoor air-conditioning of the huge ranch house. Maddie took her inside, unsnapped the leash to give Skeeter the run of the house, then stepped into the back hall bathroom to freshen up and quickly run a brush through her hair.

She was back outside on the sidelines of the dance in no time. Not five seconds after she got there, she was asked to dance. Maddie smiled and accepted, throwing herself into the dance and the festivities with a sparkling charm and enthusiasm that even she had never suspected of herself.

Linc kept track of Maddie for the next two hours, though they both went through a couple dozen partners each. She was on the warpath, that was certain, and he might have been more amused over it if he hadn't realized the hurt that was truly behind it all.

He'd come to the barbecue to see how Maddie was doing, but he'd only been able to stay away from her so long. He'd been a saint these last weeks, keeping his distance, waiting for her to find her way with everyone.

The main reason he'd done it was that he'd heard the gossip about the two of them. The giggly innuendoes about him "taming the shrew" had been bawdy and coarse, and they'd made him furious. He knew he'd had an effect on Maddie's new behavior, but he saw himself and the plane crash as the catalyst for something Maddie would have come to on her own eventually.

He'd been tough on her, he'd even dunked her in the stream, but Madison St. John's change from bitchy to sweet had nothing to do with any sudden discovery of sex or her level of sexual satisfaction. The change in her was the result of a guilty conscience and the latent good character that she'd finally been motivated to act on.

Linc had avoided her because he'd been touchy about the gossip. She'd needed time to establish the change in her attitude without a visible connection to him. Because everyone knew they'd spent the time after the crash alone—and some had concluded they'd spent the whole time wrapped in a blanket having sex—he'd hoped staying away from her would help restore her reputation.

The maneuver had worked. As far as he'd heard, the ribald remarks had stopped and people were genuinely taking note of the new Maddie. He'd meant to stay away from her tonight, too, just in case, but he'd not been able to stand seeing one more smitten male twirl her around the dance floor.

He'd reached a decision about Maddie weeks ago, and he saw no point now in extending the wait. From the looks of things tonight, if he didn't act soon, he might have to wade a sea of suitors to reclaim her attention.

Maddie excused herself from the next dance, and slipped into the house to get Skeeter for another walk. This time, she needed more time to cool off. The evening was winding down and after hours of loud music, she also needed to give her ears a rest.

She grabbed the bolero-length jacket that went with her sundress because once she cooled off, her bare arms and shoulders might feel chilled in the night air.

She sneaked Skeeter out the front, but they lingered in the side yard. Maddie leaned back against the house, thinking.

Linc hadn't approached her for a dance since that first time, but he'd easily had as many partners that night as she'd had. No matter where she saw him in the crowd, he was always someplace where he could watch her. As the night had gone on, she'd been able to track his increasingly dark frowns and occasional sharp looks. She'd not exactly set out to make him jealous, though it surprised her to think jealousy might account for the way he'd been looking at her.

Maddie had meant to demonstrate her independence, and the fact that she'd never be some needy female who'd pine away in the shadows until Linc was in the mood to spend a few odd moments with her. Now she worried that she hadn't accomplished what she'd set out to do. Whether Linc was jealous or not—and she didn't really believe she could make him jealous—it seemed certain that she'd at least earned his disapproval.

Maddie was disappointed in that. She'd wanted Linc to think well of her, and secretly, she'd wanted his approval. She might be angry with him, but she respected him. In fact, it went counter to her perception of Linc to think he was anything like the people in her life who'd abandoned her and caused her such pain. Now she began to wonder if she'd overreacted to his lack of contact these past weeks.

Linc ran a small empire of ranches and businesses and investments. The crash and all its consequences had probably complicated his life even more. While she didn't want to be ignored, she also understood that the world didn't revolve around her and her wishes.

She'd put on the little jacket and was just about to

go in, when Skeeter suddenly lunged at the end of her leash. Maddie hadn't been holding on tightly, and the loop slipped from her fingers. She started to bend down to catch the end of the leash when Skeeter bounded off, jerking it out of reach.

"Skeeter!" Annoyed with Skeeter's penchant for haring off, Maddie started after her. Skeeter led her on a merry chase, completely avoiding the crowd at the back of the house to make a wide circle that led Maddie toward the new stable.

Maddie groaned when she realized Skeeter's destination. As it turned out, the cougar wasn't the only dangerous animal the little dog had confronted in the short time Maddie had known her. Skeeter absolutely loved Caitlin's horses, barking at them, chasing them, and generally daring one of them to step on her. It was all a fun game for Skeeter, and it surprised Maddie that all but a couple of the more spirited horses patiently regarded the yippy little dog as an interesting nuisance.

Skeeter went straight to the stall of her favorite, who happened to be Caitlin's black gelding. The stable lights were dimmed, but Maddie could see clearly the length of the stable aisle to the black's stall near the opposite end. Skeeter was jumping on the stall gate, yapping wildly.

Maddie rushed down the aisle and swept the dog up. "Shame on you, naughty girl," she scolded gently and held Skeeter up to frown into her tiny face.

The gelding put his head over the stall gate and pushed his nose toward Skeeter. Skeeter squirmed wildly, trying to touch her nose to the horse's. The gelding waited until Skeeter got close, then blew out a deep breath of air that riffled the hair on the dog's face. Skeeter sneezed and gave an eager little groan that made Maddie laugh.

Linc's voice from down the aisle gave her a start.

"She's made a habit of daring dangerous animals."

Maddie glanced over her shoulder, then turned, pulling Skeeter close to her. She realized the gesture was a protective one, but she couldn't help it.

"She's a lot like you."

The low words sent a vibration of alarm and excitement through her. Linc was still a few feet away, but he came toward her with the loose cowboy walk that was nothing less than a macho Texas swagger. The impression of dangerous, virile male was strong and her heart went wild.

She thought about that night at the stream. The night when she'd gone over the line with Linc and he'd moved toward her with the same hint of menace that he did now. She cuddled Skeeter close and the little dog squirmed in her arms.

But, oh, how wonderfully sexy he looked! His black Stetson shadowing his face—his strong, ruggedly handsome face—his broad shoulders, his lean waist and hips, his powerful thighs. And the power and poetry of the easy way he moved, the ripple and bunch and release of hard muscle and sleek sinew.

The strong, profound memory of what that big hard body had felt like against hers sent an earthquake of reaction through her followed by the hot lava of yearning and anticipation. Maddie was so completely disrupted that she couldn't speak.

Skeeter was squirming madly, eager to get Linc's attention. Her excited yip made his dark, dark gaze drop. Maddie's breath caught because he'd almost reached her and now he loomed close, making her aware of her petite height and feminine fragility. But then he stopped and simply plucked the little dog out of her arms.

She felt a tiny break in the tension between them when Linc smiled at the dog and said a few gruff words to her before he set her on a nearby hay bale. He hooked the end of her leash on the handle of the tack room door.

When he turned back to Maddie, her breath caught and she eased back a half step. The look on his face was fierce, and his dark eyes were positively smoldering.

"Remember what I told you before? How almost every word outta your mouth aims a challenge?"

Maddie didn't answer, but felt her eyes go rounder.

"Well, lady," he drawled, his voice going so low and sexy that she felt it stroke through her insides like a velvet glove, "you finally threw down the last gauntlet."

He reached for her then. Maddie took a hasty step back and put up her hands to ward him off, though she didn't know why. She trusted him not to hurt her, but his sexual intensity was so overpowering that she felt faint. Linc caught her wrist so suddenly that she gave a little gasp.

Electricity sizzled along every nerve in her body, sending a bright charge through every atom. She pressed her free hand against his chest because his nearness seemed to steal the air from her lungs.

"What? Nothing to say?" A slow smile crossed

his handsome mouth. "No declarations? No little *how dare you's?*"

Maddie tried to pull back, but Linc's fingers tightened gently. His grip didn't hurt, but it was unbreakable.

"Smell that fresh clean hay overhead?"

The low question confused her a moment and she automatically glanced up at the stable ceiling that was the floor of the massive loft. But when her gaze came down and connected with his, she realized his intent. Her eyes went even rounder and she tried to pull back in earnest.

"You *wouldn't!*"

Maddie cringed inwardly at the scandalized emphasis she'd put on the words. She also realized that Linc had been waiting for a response from her along those lines. Taken another way, it was a dare, and when that dawned on Maddie, her soft, "No," was little more than a thready whisper.

"Always wanted to carry some little blonde into a loft and make mad, crazy love to her. Reckon I'll never have a better chance."

Linc leaned down, placed his shoulder against her waist, and used his light grip on her wrist to bend her over his back. Then he straightened and turned to walk briskly to the ladder partway down the aisle. Skeeter went crazy, yipping herself nearly hoarse.

Maddie gasped, bracing her free hand on Linc's back to lever herself upright. He'd tossed her over his shoulder and was carrying her like a sack of feed! Her! Madison St. John! Who prided herself on her dignified, ladylike composure—even if she hadn't always behaved nicely!

Hadn't she seen this on a *Bonanza* episode? Had
Marshall Matt on *Gunsmoke* ever done this to Miss
Kitty? Maybe she'd seen Nick Barkley do it to some
woman on *The Big Valley*—maybe all three! Now
that she was living it, she realized she might have
seen some macho cowboy on every western in the
history of television throw some woman over his
shoulder and head for someplace to kiss her.

John Wayne had carried his share of women like
this, and she wondered hysterically if the Duke had
ever carried his women any other way. If he had, she
couldn't remember it now. The shocking surprise of
it all, the complete absurdity of her wild thoughts—
startled a giggle out of her.

"No! Linc, please! Put me down!" Her protests
were spoiled by a string of compulsive little giggles
that interrupted each phrase. When she felt Linc start
up the ladder, she sobered and tried again, but
Skeeter's yips turned to rabid little growls and
Maddie dissolved into another fit of giggles.

Linc's gruff, "Watch your head," made her give a
wary "Eaaa!" as she hugged close to his back. She
was dizzy now from being carried head-down, and by
the time Linc reached the top of the ladder and
stepped onto the raw wood of the loft, she was completely disoriented. She felt him climb high on the
hay bales, and then she was lifted and guided through
the air to a safe landing on her back.

Linc followed her down, trapping her beneath him
with her wrists manacled by her head. His lips
swooped down to hers, but she was so caught up in
euphoric giggles that she couldn't keep her lips to-

gether solidly enough for a decent kiss. She finally turned her head as he pulled back.

"You little hellion. Damn if you're not a jack-in-the-box of surprises." The gruff affection of Linc's words was like a rain of sweetness on her heart.

"I made up my mind to have you, Maddie," he went on and the sudden seriousness of his words began to sober her. She turned her head to look up into the dark turbulence in his eyes. Desire, sincerity, and stark, intense affection. And mixed in with it all was a solemnity that told her this was it, this was everything she'd hoped for, everything she'd needed, everything her heart had craved.

"I haven't waited long to have you, but it feels like I've waited years. I want to marry you, Madison St. John. I realize I'm not the cultured, refined man you mighta ha—"

Linc's hands had loosened on her wrists and she jerked them free to grab his shoulders and lift her head to press her lips solidly against his. Linc hesitated, then sank down against her, his mouth taking over in a deep, soul-stealing kiss so carnal that Maddie was certain the hay would burst into flames around them.

Linc at last drew back, his breath as ragged as hers. "I love you, Maddie, please marry me."

Maddie laid her shaking palm against his lean jaw and lightly stroked it. "Oh, Linc, I love you so much. I'll marry you whenever you say."

Linc's mouth shifted into a smile. "And this from the woman who told me not three hours ago that she'd never give me absolute power over her or allow me to dictate how she lives her life."

Maddie reached up to gently grab a handful of his hair to give it a playful tug. "Don't read so much into one teensy concession, cowboy. Besides, it's probably the last say you'll ever get."

"I'll take my chances, darlin'."

And then he kissed her.

Somewhere below them, Skeeter gave up trying to get anyone's attention. The black gelding put his head over the stall door and eyed the little dog. Some cross-species communication took place. Skeeter walked to the edge of the hay bale, caught the leash in her tiny teeth, then reared up on her hind legs to walk her front feet up the wall.

Eventually, she worked the loop off the tack room doorknob, then jumped off the hay bale to scamper off to visit her equine friend. And brag about the success of the scheme that had brought her two favorite humans together.

# EPILOGUE

SIX WEEKS LATER, Maddie became Mrs. Lincoln Coryell before two hundred guests, in a large, formal ceremony on the LC Ranch's back patio and lawn. Her cousin, Caitlin, was the matron of honor. Caitlin's husband, Reno, was Linc's best man.

Skeeter caused a minor disruption when someone forgot to close a door at the ranch house, and she came tearing up the aisle between the guests to join the ceremony. Nimbly eluding the best man's effort to grab her, Skeeter sat down at the minister's feet to gaze up in doggie delight at the chagrined bride and patient groom.

After the laughter died down, Maddie and Linc pledged their love and their lives to each other. When the minister introduced them to the guests as husband and wife, Skeeter joined the lineup, then jauntily followed them down the aisle to the reception.

A year later, within a day of each other at the Coulter City Hospital, Maddie Coryell and Caitlin Duvall gave birth to daughters. It was a profound moment for them both. For Caitlin, who had lost her mother, the birth of her daughter had an added poignancy and joy. She would also become the mother of two sons.

For Maddie, who never heard from her mother after the plane crash, the birth of her daughter was healing. She would never have the close, loving relationship with her mother that she'd always hungered for, but the moment she gazed down into her infant's eyes, she realized that with her new daughter, she was being given a second chance to fill that sad, lonely space in her heart.

And the deep bond between the two cousins became even more precious as they realized that their daughters would not only grow up dearly loved by mothers and fathers who loved each other, but that the two tiny cousins would, in their generation, repeat the same close relationship that their mothers would have all their lives.

Skeeter was completely devoted to Maddie's little girl, who became her co-conspirator. As did the two daughters who came later.

# ☙ *Harlequin Romance*®

We're proud to announce the "birth" of a brand-
new series full of babies, bachelors and happy-
ever-afters: ***Daddy Boom***. Meet gorgeous heroes
who are about to discover that there's a first time
for everything—even fatherhood!

We'll be bringing you one deliciously cute
***Daddy Boom*** title every other month in 1999.
Books in this series are:

### Who says bachelors and babies don't mix?

Available wherever Harlequin books are sold.

**HARLEQUIN**®
*Makes any time special.*™

# ℋarlequin Romance®

**brings you four very special weddings to remember in our new series:**

*True love is worth waiting for....*

Look out for the following titles by some of your favorite authors:

**August 1999—SHOTGUN BRIDEGROOM #3564**
**Day Leclaire**
Everyone is determined to protect Annie's good name and ensure that bad boy Sam's seduction attempts don't end in the bedroom—but begin with a wedding!

**September 1999—A WEDDING WORTH WAITING FOR #3569**
**Jessica Steele**
Karrie was smitten by boss Farne Maitland. But she was determined to be a virgin bride. There was only one solution: marry and quickly!

**October 1999—MARRYING MR. RIGHT #3573**
**Carolyn Greene**
Greg was wrongly arrested on his wedding night for something he didn't do! Now he's about to reclaim his virgin bride when he discovers Christina's intention to marry someone else....

**November 1999—AN INNOCENT BRIDE #3577**
**Betty Neels**
Katrina didn't know it yet but Simon Glenville, the wonderful doctor who'd cared for her sick aunt, was in love with her. When the time was right, he was going to propose....

*Available wherever Harlequin books are sold.*

# Every Man Has His Price!

# HEART OF THE WEST

## At the heart of the West there are a dozen rugged bachelors—up for auction!

## This August 1999, look for *Courting Callie* by **Lynn Erickson**

If Mase Lebow testifies at a high-profile trial, he knows his six-year-old son, Joey, will pay. Mase decides to hide his son at Callie Thorpe's ranch, out of harm's way. Callie, of course, has no idea why Joey is really there, and falling in love with his tight-lipped father is a definite inconvenience.

**Each book features a sexy new bachelor up for grabs—and a woman determined to rope him in!**

*Available August 1999 at your favorite retail outlet.*

**HARLEQUIN®**
*Makes any time special* ™

Look us up on-line at: http://www.romance.net

PHHOW2

# ℋarlequin ℛomance®

## Coming Next Month

**#3563  MAKING MR RIGHT  Val Daniels**
Giving Parker Chaney advice on how to become her sister's Mr Right
was hard for Cindy when she herself had been secretly in love with him
for years! But soon Parker seemed more interested in what *she* was
looking for in a husband. Could Cindy hope to be more than the sister
of the bride after all?

**#3564  SHOTGUN BRIDEGROOM  Day Leclaire**
Seven years ago Sam was going to elope with Annie; instead he was run
out of town. Now he's back, and he wants Annie. But the whole town is
determined to protect her good name, and ensure that Sam doesn't
have his wicked way with Annie until they are married!

**White Weddings:** *True love is worth waiting for...*

**#3565  BRIDE INCLUDED  Janelle Denison**
Eleven years ago Seth left Josie brokenhearted—and pregnant! Now
he's back—to claim not only Josie's family home but Josie, too! It
seems her father gambled both on a game of cards! Now Josie must
either give up her home or marry a man she told herself she no longer
cared about.

**Back to the Ranch:** *How the West is won...and wooed!*

**#3566  THE DADDY DILEMMA  Kate Denton**
Attorney Mackie Smith sets out determined to win custody of
Gordon Galloway's little daughter on behalf of his ex-wife. But it is
hard keeping her mind on the job when she realizes that adorable baby
Ashley *belongs* with her even more adorable daddy—and that she's
fallen for them both!

**Daddy Boom:** *Who says bachelors and babies don't mix?*